FiENDISH

WAYS

Damaged Devils #5

Charity Parkerson

Punk & Sissy Publications

COPYRIGHT

—Warning: This book is intended for readers over the age of 18. Some of my books contain allusions to past abuse and trauma.

Editor: BZ Hercules & Consultants

Cover art: Temptation Creations

CONTENTS

Author Note

THIS IS A DARK romance series filled with possible triggers. If you need a list, you can skip to the content warning after the About the Author page or check my website: charityparkerson.com/damaged-devils

INTRODUCTION

IN A MOMENT OF rare heroism, Cree rescued a beautiful blond stray. It was the dumbest move he's ever made.

A few months back, while tailing someone for his boss, Cree rolled right into a domestic dispute. As someone raised by monsters, he can't stand idly by while a tiny sprite gets beaten down by a behemoth. When he stepped in, he planned to take care of business and move along. Instead, he walks face first into the greatest love of his life... and the thing that might completely destroy him.

Nebraska's whole life has been exhausting. When he ends up living with complete strangers, hundreds of miles from home, he should be terrified. Instead, it's the lightest he's felt in years. The problem is they're all killers and generally bad men. He knows he's not free to leave. Not alive, anyway. Yet Nebraska has never felt safer, and he can't shake the one heated gaze that follows him everywhere. He's never been happier. Now all he has to do is survive... and make his surly bodyguard fall in love with him. No pressure.

Fiendish Ways is the fifth book in Charity Parkerson's Damaged Devils series. These are dark romance stories with crime lords, assassins, and sociopaths who find their hearts. They are best enjoyed when read in order.

CHAPTER ONE

HOW IT BEGAN...

Three months ago.

His face stung. Nebraska already knew from experience he wouldn't be able to see out of his left eye by the end of the day. As always, he didn't even know what set off his dad's tirade. Nebraska had just been doing as told, trying to help sort through their things in storage. Then his dad had mumbled to himself about Nebraska being useless. Nebraska had immediately decided to walk away. He had known exactly where things would go from there. Hate-filled words had been hurled at his back. Boxes started flying. One hit him in the back of neck and head, unbalancing him. Then his dad's fists had started flying. The way they always did.

Nebraska didn't fight back. That never failed to make things worse. He tried to stay still, calm, and hope things ended fast. His dad disappeared. Nebraska blinked. He was still too disoriented to focus. His gaze moved around the room, hunting for the next strike. Except his dad was three feet off the ground. A beefy arm choked the life from him. His purple face got darker by the second. He flailed helplessly against the man who held him with ease. Nebraska couldn't move. All he could do was stare. His dad was huge. No one ever challenged him. This guy was bigger. Sweat didn't even coat his brow from the struggle.

The man's blue gaze locked onto Nebraska. He looked cold. A chill ran down Nebraska's spine. "Are you okay?"

Even though it wasn't true, Nebraska nodded.

"Good. Please step outside."

He was so calm. So polite. Nebraska didn't even hesitate to do as he asked. His feet carried him outside. Something tickled his face. Nebraska brushed it away and realized he was bleeding. With no other choice, he peeled off his shirt and used it to pinch his nose. He always had the worst nosebleeds once they started. They took forever to stop. His thoughts were strange. They were scattered but calm. In his heart, Nebraska understood that only feet away, some guy probably killed his father. Maybe it was shock, but Nebraska felt nothing. He was completely unbothered. Harold James had been begging to die badly for as long as Nebraska could recall. He was violent and heartless. When Nebraska's mom had died, and he had been sent to live with his dad, he had tried begging for foster care. His parents had been divorced for a reason. There had been a restraining order for a reason. His dad hadn't been given visitation for a reason. No one listened. CPS was overworked and the foster care system already had their hands full. Nebraska had a place to go, so that was where he went. Now he was nineteen and could have left last year, except no, he couldn't.

Harold wouldn't let him go. So Nebraska felt nothing.

It seemed as if hours had passed before his savior reappeared. He quietly closed the door on the storage unit before meeting Nebraska's stare. "What's your name?"

"Nebraska," Nebraska mumbled around the shirt.

The man moved closer. He took the shirt from Nebraska and checked beneath. With the softest touch, he wiped Nebraska's face. "I'm Cree. You weren't part of my plan today, Nebraska. I still have a job to do. You're not bleeding any longer." He didn't back away. Nebraska kept staring up at him, mesmerized, as Cree spoke. "I can't leave you behind. For one, you've seen my face. Second, if this is a common occurrence, you'll be the first person the cops question when they can't find this piece of shit."

"Oh." Nebraska didn't know what else to say. "I doubt anyone except the bar owner down the street will miss him. He hasn't worked in years, and he doesn't have any friends."

Cree nodded. "Still. I'm not a man who takes chances... or hostages. Will you willing get in the SUV behind you?"

Nebraska glanced over his shoulder. A black SUV sat parked at his back. His gaze slid back to the giant who saved him. "Yes." It was funny. Nebraska knew it was likely the man intended to kill him and dispose of his body. Yet he still agreed. He also wasn't scared, but Nebraska didn't move. His gaze refused to give up the sight of Cree.

Cree's features softened.

The air left Nebraska's lungs in a stuttering whoosh.

"You're safe now."

Was he? Because Nebraska didn't care at all. He just wanted to stay with Cree.

CHAPTER TWO

PRESENT DAY...

Nebraska's best friend growing up, Amelia, had always said he was too innocent and trusting. She claimed he would end up dead in a ditch someday. If Nebraska's dad hadn't destroyed their friendship, she would probably chastise him for his current living situation. He had been staying with complete strangers nearly five hundred miles from everything he knew for three months now.

They hadn't killed him and left him in a ditch yet.

The thing about him was, it wasn't that he was innocent and trusting. That was something Amelia had never understood. He had seen too much heartache to be truly innocent, and he wasn't here because he had been too trusting. Nebraska was desperate. Being at absolute rock bottom changed a person's outlook. He didn't have the luxury to worry about trust. Nebraska needed to survive, and he couldn't leave Cree. Not that he thought he would be allowed to leave anyhow.

Three men crowded into the kitchen where Nebraska enjoyed his cereal. All three had visible weapons. Nebraska tucked in closer to his bowl and ignored their chatter. The house belonged to Archer Woods. From what Nebraska gathered in his three-month stay, Cree was Archer's bodyguard. He didn't know why he needed guarding. Nebraska didn't ask, and no one offered explanations. He considered taking his cereal to his room. Everyone ignored him. Nebraska got more nervous by the second. He tried making himself smaller. Everyone was so fucking big. Big men with weapons reminded him too much of his dad. Nebraska had learned years ago to be quiet and invisible. He kept his eyes on his bowl.

Warms hands landed on his shoulders. Nebraska drew a deep breath. He hadn't seen Cree in a few days. Cree had gone out of town with Archer. Nebraska didn't know where. He never asked questions. But he immediately recognized Cree's hands and Nebraska had missed them. Nebraska could never say that.

Warm lips moved closer to his ear. "Why are you eating breakfast at one o'clock in the afternoon?"

Nebraska fought a smile. "The thought of regular food made me feel sick."

Cree pulled out the chair beside him and met his stare. Those blue eyes owned him. "Are you having another Crohn's flare up?"

It was embarrassing, but Cree had found him on the floor, curled up and crying a month after moving him in. From there, Cree had been privy to all of Nebraska's embarrassing medical issues. He nodded. "It's not so bad this time, but I'm having trouble eating."

"Have you been taking your meds?"

Nebraska shook his head. "I ran out before you left town, and I didn't have any way to get them filled."

Irritation crossed Cree's features. "Why didn't you say something?"

Nebraska went back to staring at his cereal. The pain in his stomach was building to unbearable again, making him sensitive. "Archer doesn't like it when I bother you. Plus, I already feel like a burden."

Cree pushed Nebraska's bowl away, forcing him to look Cree's way. "Come on. Let's take care of this before you're incapacitated."

"You just got home."

Cree made a show of dropping his gaze to the way Nebraska white-knuckled the edge of the table. Nebraska pried his fingers away and clasped his hands in his lap. A cold sweat coated his skin. With a shake of his head, Cree easily plucked Nebraska from his chair and headed down the hall. He paused as he passed a housekeeper.

"Will you grab an ice pack for me?"

The lady nodded, and Cree kept moving. "You relax with an ice pack, and I'll run to the pharmacy."

Nebraska stared up at Cree from his spot in Cree's arms. "Always the hero."

Cree snorted.

Nebraska hid a smile against Cree's chest at the sound. Just being in Cree's arms made him feel a tad better. He knew Cree would fix everything. That was what Cree did. He made Nebraska better.

Even though Cree didn't know how to say it, he resented the days of working that took him away from Nebraska. They had a unique relationship. From the moment Cree brought Nebraska home, he had become like a dragon hoarding his treasure—or a white lady with a stray dog. He wanted to put Nebraska in soft pajamas and give him treats.

Cree couldn't explain what happened or when. At first, Cree had only felt mild pity for Nebraska. Then he had noticed Nebraska's green eyes were pretty in the sunlight and his curly hair looked soft. His first breaking point had been the day he found Nebraska curled in a tight ball and silently crying. Nebraska had refused to make a sound, as if he worried being any sort of nuisance would get him hurt. Cree had immediately called in a private doctor. He had also hovered like an old mother hen the entire time. Cree didn't like to talk about that, while Archer loved bringing up that part. Now Nebraska hurt again, and Cree hated it. He had to make him better.

Cree headed up the stairs and to his bedroom. He had kept Nebraska in his room since bringing him home. That had been an order straight from Archer. If Cree wanted to keep Nebraska—like a stray dog—he had to keep the boy in his room, out of everyone's hair, and watch him so he didn't escape. They couldn't risk Nebraska telling anyone anything he saw there. Cree knew better, though. Nebraska had nowhere to go, no money, and no family. He wouldn't run away. Still, Cree did as told. He set Nebraska on the bed they shared and then plugged in the heating pad. Nebraska needed to do ice for a few minutes first and then rotate to heat. While that might not work for everyone, that seemed to work best for Nebraska until Cree could get meds in him. They had a lot of practice trying different things to soothe his pain. It had taken weeks for Nebraska to find relief from the pills. He supposed it had to build up in his system, but still, that whole month had been hell.

Someone knocked on the door. Cree raced to answer. Thankfully, it was the ice pack he requested. Cree snagged it and mumbled his thanks before quickly returning to Nebraska's side. He passed it Nebraska's way, since he didn't know where the worst of the pain was located.

Nebraska flashed him a grateful smile.

Cree pulled out his phone and called in a favor.

King answered on the third ring. "Hello?"

"Hey, King. Can I get you to make a pharmacy run for me?"

"Sure. I'm already at the store for Angel."

"Thank God. Can you grab Nebraska's script? He's in a lot of pain."

"Sure. There are also some pain meds in my room, if he needs them."

"Thanks. I'll check your stash."

"See you in a few."

King disconnected the call and Cree put his phone in his pocket. "I'll be right back." He rushed from the room and across the hall to King's room. King hadn't been living with them for long. Most of his things were still in boxes. He had been hired—at first—to protect one of Archer's assets. Since that job ended, he had come to live with Archer to give Cree more time off during the week. Cree appreciated the help. Even though Archer didn't jet around the country the way he had before he married, Cree still had to be on duty way more than most before King came onboard. Cree liked the guy, but King did like his pills. Not only was Cree not one to judge, but he was also grateful today. He easily found something strong to help Nebraska. Cree hurried back to their room.

After grabbing a bottle of water from the fridge in their room, he hurried back to Nebraska's side. "Here. Take one of these."

Proving how much pain he was in, Nebraska didn't question a thing. He swallowed the pill and settled back down. "Thank you."

Cree didn't need to be thanked. He needed Nebraska to get better. "Scoot over."

Nebraska winced as he made room for Cree beside him. Cree settled on his side next to Nebraska and gently rubbed the spot below the ice pack. He felt how shallow Nebraska's breaths were, as if he measured each one to mitigate the pain.

Cree pressed his lips to Nebraska's temple. "Just relax. Close your eyes. I've got you."

"This has to be one of the most embarrassing pains in the world and you always treat me like... I don't know how to explain it. Like it's not."

That was on Nebraska's youth. Everyone else knew there was no reason for Nebraska to be embarrassed. Cree didn't say that. "It's not. I know you're in severe pain. It doesn't matter what causes it. I'm here to help."

"Thank God."

Cree smiled at the open relief in Nebraska's voice. That was what made him Cree's biggest addiction. He had never been the hero. Cree had been born into poverty and sold to an assassin program. After being tortured into becoming a hired killer, he had done the job he had been trained to do. He protected crime lords, and killed and tortured people. Cree wasn't the protagonist. He was the villain. Not with Nebraska. For the first time, Cree had rescued someone and kept him safe. He had nurtured life. Nebraska never looked at him with fear. He gave Cree a place to be soft.

Cree heard Nebraska's breathing deepen. The ice pack slipped. Cree snagged it and set it aside before dragging the heating pad across Nebraska's stomach. He went back to holding him and stole his chance to stare. Nebraska was adorable. He always filled Cree's chest and melted him. There was a smattering of light freckles across the bridge of Nebraska's nose. He looked incredibly young and vulnerable. Nebraska was those things. Cree had over twenty years on the guy. No doubt Nebraska only saw him as a father figure. Cree told himself that was for the best. He was a bad person and Nebraska deserved someone kind. Still, Cree enjoyed these moments when he got to quietly dream. No one and nothing else brought him peace. Holding Nebraska gave him that. Cree didn't want their time together to end.

The pain had—thankfully—passed. Between the pain meds and King slipping into the room to give him his Crohn's medication, Nebraska felt much better. For at least an hour, Nebraska savored watching Cree sleep. On his side, facing Cree, Nebraska's gaze stayed locked on

Cree. Even in his sleep, he was hard. Cree probably scared small children. Nebraska wondered how many people Cree had killed. He didn't doubt it had been several. Nebraska also wondered what it said about him he didn't care. He had never felt safer.

Part of Nebraska wanted to wake Cree so those sexy blue eyes could focus on him. The rest of Nebraska dreaded the moment Cree came awake and abandoned him again. Cree seemed to spend less and less time with him all the time.

Nebraska's gaze moved down Cree's body. His dress shirt was open at the collar. A hint of muscular chest peeked out, making Nebraska's mouth water. That was another thing. Cree made him very, very horny, and it was torture being this close to touching him. Nebraska shared his bed—platonically. They slept inches apart, and Nebraska never saw Cree as much as talking to anyone else. There were no women or men, as far as Nebraska could tell. Nebraska assumed Cree did those things on the nights he was out of town with Archer. In fact, he wondered if it was Archer who shared his bed. Archer seemed to genuinely love his husband. Nebraska didn't know if that mattered. He had never been exposed to a healthy relationship. Maybe everyone cheated. It ate at Nebraska, thinking of Cree touching anyone else.

Without a plan, Nebraska quietly scooted closer. He wanted to touch Cree. It was a sickness in his blood. Thanks to his psycho father, Nebraska had never gotten much of a chance to date. He had never had sex with anyone. Nebraska daydreamed more than could be considered healthy. It was always the same body covering his in his mind. One of the most terrifying parts was, he didn't really know if Cree was gay. Archer obviously was, and it seemed like they only associated with gay men, but he hadn't actually seen Cree show interest in anyone. He always freely touched Nebraska, but Nebraska had a bad feeling that was a fatherly affection. There was nothing familial about the way Nebraska felt. He wanted to blow cum all over Cree's body. Nebraska wanted to put Cree's dick in his mouth and learn how to give head. He knew Cree would be a patient teacher. Desire ate at his brain—like scratching rats. He couldn't stop thinking about Cree's cock. Nebraska went to ridiculous lengths to accidentally touch it. Maybe he would do that now.

Nebraska eased even closer. His gaze stayed locked on Cree's open collar. Saliva filled his mouth. He had to taste that spot. His dick was hard and leaking inside his shorts. He set his hand on Cree's side, savoring his hard body as he inched closer. His lips were a hairsbreadth from Cree's throat. He felt Cree stir. Nebraska went still. With his eyes closed, he focused on keeping his breathing even. After a moment of feigning sleep, Cree's body relaxed. His breathing evened out again. Nebraska chanced a glance at his face. He was asleep.

With freedom restored, Nebraska touched his lips to Cree's throat. Painful longing rose in Nebraska's chest. He had never wanted anything in his life as badly as he craved Cree. His lips moved lower. He risked a small lick. Nebraska fought a moan as salt coated his tongue. Holy shit. He so badly wanted to set his dick free and rub it against Cree's skin. Nebraska had never felt so desperate or twisted.

A loud banging sounded on the door.

Nebraska scrambled away.

"Archer and Angel are going out."

Nebraska risked a quick peek at Cree. His blue gaze was locked on Nebraska's face. His cheeks were flushed, making his eyes seem that much bluer. He didn't say a word or look disoriented. For a moment, Nebraska toyed with a terrible thought. Had Cree been awake? How horrifying.

CHAPTER THREE

CREE COULDN'T THINK STRAIGHT tonight. He definitely didn't want to be sitting at dinner with Angel and Archer right now. Leaving Nebraska behind in a warm bed had been hell, especially after that sneaky kiss. It wasn't the first time Cree had caught Nebraska getting close while they slept. The first few times, he had brushed it off as Nebraska dreaming or unaware it was Cree. Today had felt different. Nebraska had definitely feigned sleep when he thought Cree might catch him. Cree felt at a crossroads. On one hand, he absolutely wanted to touch Nebraska. On the other, Cree must seem like the only choice for Nebraska... or worse, Stockholm Syndrome.

"We need to address the staffing shortage. Since the association of demons closed up shop, we don't have the same steady stream of members looking for work."

"Closed up shop" was a nice way of saying one of their trained assassins murdered them.

Archer kept talking, oblivious to Cree finding humor in his words. "We can't risk accidentally hiring a government agent."

Archer had to add that "accidentally" since they had just purposely let an ex-FBI agent into their midst.

"It's getting harder to find the right people. If anyone has any suggestions or knows anyone looking for work."

"What about Nebraska?" The words were out before Cree could stop himself.

Archer's laughing gaze moved Cree's way. "No offense, but Nebraska doesn't exactly look like he could handle himself."

Cree nodded. The idea grew on him. If Nebraska didn't have to depend on Cree, then Cree would know if Nebraska genuinely wanted him. "Exactly. No one would suspect him. He's tiny. If it appeared he was the only person with you, your enemies wouldn't hesitate to show themselves. There's no way any-one would think Nebraska was protec-tion. They'd probably think you didn't have any guards with you because you were hiding an affair or some shit. He's the perfect cover slash bait."

Archer eyed him. He was smart. No doubt he saw right through Cree, but there was no way Archer could deny it was a good plan. After a moment, Archer sighed. "Fine. Put him on the payroll, but he's your responsibility. You have to train him. I don't need anyone else distracted by your pet."

Cree nodded. He could handle things alone. Plus, Cree didn't want anyone else spending time with Nebraska anyhow. The guy belonged to him. Stockholm Syndrome or not. Nebraska was his.

"How's Nebraska feeling?" King's quietly spoken question pulled Cree from his thoughts.

His gaze slid King's way. His dark hair framed his face. His whiskey-colored eyes held a hint of genuine concern. Considering King had been raised the same as Cree and enjoyed killing people, his inquiry meant more than if it came from anyone else. King had no reason to care other than he did. "He's doing better. Thanks for helping out earlier. He drives me crazy when he lets things get worse than they need to be, simply because he's too stubborn to ask for help."

"He loves you. He doesn't want to be a burden."

Cree blinked. Honestly, it might have been more of a flinch. He couldn't tell. "He's a kid."

King snorted hard enough it had to hurt. "Okay. If you're blind, I'm not. I can take him off your hands."

For a moment, Cree lost vision in his right eye. Rage threatened to make him do something he might or might not regret.

A bright smile lit King's face. "That's what I thought. Stop being dumb and blind. That *kid* lives for you."

Fuck. It hadn't occurred to Cree he might have competition among the other men in the house. He should have seen it, though. Nebraska was beautiful. Of course, other people had noticed. Cree needed to step up his game. Otherwise, Nebraska might slip away.

All Nebraska could do was stare at Cree in horror. Cree obviously believed Nebraska working for Archer was a dream position. All Nebraska heard was he would get his ass kicked. Again.

"You do realize I spent my entire life getting my ass handed to me. Now you want me to let you fight me?"

Cree rolled his eyes. "You won't get hurt. I'll teach you how to defend yourself."

Nebraska nodded. He tried hiding his feelings behind a mask. Honestly, he was pretty damn good at hiding hurt. He had been doing it his whole life. "If this is what you want." There. That sounded neutral enough. In truth, Nebraska was silently panicking. This felt a lot like Cree looked for a way to get out from underneath caring for him. That was fair. Nebraska had known he couldn't depend on Cree forever. This was for the best.

"You don't want this."

Damn. Nebraska tried harder at Cree's defeated-sounding statement. He clasped his hands and dug his short fingernails into his palm, trying to distract himself from the pains in his chest. "Obviously, I have to do something. It's not like I can stay holed up in your bedroom forever. If this is what you want, then it's whatever. I trust you."

Cree's gaze dropped to Nebraska's clasped hands. "You don't believe that I'll keep you safe."

Nebraska forced his hands to unclench. "Please stop. I've already agreed."

With his ass half perched on the dresser, Cree stared at Nebraska on the bed where he had been lazily hanging out all night. King had brought him food before Cree left and Nebraska had watched movies. Maybe he needed to do something. He supposed he probably looked useless to Cree. It was no wonder Cree didn't want him. The more he mulled over the situation, the more he thought he might hyperventilate. It was never good for him to be alone with his thoughts.

Nebraska couldn't look directly at Cree anymore. "Please stop staring at me. I know I'm a disappointment. I'll do what you want."

"I would never force you and I could never be disappointed in you."

The soft way Cree spoke had Nebraska's shoulders relaxing. He chanced another quick glance Cree's way.

Cree stood. "Come on. Let me show you how to make this fun." He pulled Nebraska to his feet before he could argue.

With his hand in Cree's, Nebraska couldn't pull away. He craved being touched too badly. Cree moved to the small sitting room area inside his bedroom. He pushed the settee and coffee table aside, making space, and then he turned Nebraska's way.

"Okay. Attack me."

A laugh burbled in Nebraska's throat. "What?"

Cree gave him a sharp nod. "You heard me. Try to tackle me."

"I'll pass. I'm not like the guys around here. I lack your..." Nebraska fought for a way to describe what they got up to without insulting Cree. "Your fiendish ways," he finally said with a nod.

A huge smile lit Cree's face. "Fiendish ways. I like that. Still. Just trust me, okay? Try to come at me."

"No, thank you."

Cree huffed. "At least try to punch me."

Nebraska shook his head. "I'm a lover. Not a fighter."

"You've been here three months. I don't think you're either."

Ouch. That cut deep. "Then don't bother with me." He turned away. Maybe he should try to leave. It seemed like it might be time. Hurt and anger boiled inside Nebraska.

Cree grabbed his shoulder. "Don't—"

PTSD hit so hard and fast, Nebraska saw red. Nebraska reacted out of pure survival. He turned and swung. His fist connected. It hurt more than he expected, snapping him from his moment of terror.

Cree jumped back and covered his eye. He turned away and sat on the settee. Nebraska couldn't tell if he had hurt Cree that badly or if Cree tried getting his temper under control. Either thought made Nebraska feel sick.

He followed Cree. "Oh, my God. Are you okay? I'm so sorry." He straddled Cree's lap without thinking and tried prying Cree's hand away from his face. "Let me see. I'm sorry. Let me see."

Cree dropped his hand. His eye was red and watering.

Nebraska's heart tried turning a cartwheel in his chest. "Holy shit. I feel terrible." In his growing panic, Nebraska kissed Cree's eye, as if he could make it better. When he realized what he had done, Nebraska froze with his lips pressed to the corner of Cree's eye. His heart skipped a beat and then raced. Nebraska didn't know what to do. He knew he should pull away, but he didn't.

Then Cree's arms encircled him. His hands slid up Nebraska's back, urging him closer.

Nebraska's lips moved lower. He kissed Cree's cheek. His heart beat so hard and fast, he couldn't get oxygen to his brain. Before he knew what happened, his mouth landed on the corner of Cree's mouth. For a moment, neither of them moved. Then Cree turned his head. Their lips met. Nebraska sucked in a ragged breath. The world exploded into passion. Cree's tongue filled Nebraska's mouth. Everything ceased to exist except Cree. His kiss was everything Nebraska expected. He was rough and hungry. Cree treated Nebraska like he had been waiting his entire life to kiss him. Nebraska's eyes burned behind his closed lids. Until that moment, he hadn't realized the depths of his longing. He hadn't realized how badly he wanted to be loved.

"You should stop me," Cree said between kisses.

Nebraska ignored Cree's ridiculous claim. He couldn't get enough.

"Tell me no, Nebraska. I'm serious. You're a good person. I'm not. You don't want this."

Cree's half-hearted objections had Nebraska pulling away. "It's okay. You don't have to spare my feelings. I know you could have anyone."

"No. You could have anyone. I don't want you to settle for me because you're trapped here."

A laugh burst from Nebraska without his permission. "Do you think I'm trapped here? I could've chosen to leave at any time. Maybe someone would've been ordered to kill me, but I'm not afraid of that. I'm afraid of spending the rest of my life every bit as unloved as when you found me."

Nebraska climbed from Cree's lap. He wouldn't force this. Cree had kissed him back. That was more than Nebraska ever dreamed. He wouldn't hurt his own feelings by trying for more.

"Come on. Show me whatever you planned to show me. It seems I've outstayed my welcome. I may as well have a job."

Cree snagged his waist before he got away. Nebraska found himself trapped between Cree's knees and inside his unbreakable hold. His intense gaze held Nebraska's stare. "Don't walk away thinking I don't want you, because I do. You're all I want. I just need to know I'm really what you want."

All of Cree's denials made Nebraska wonder who he really tried to convince. Nebraska needed room to think. "I need air." Nebraska untangled himself and headed for the bedroom door with his heart in his throat. He was so confused. Cree kissed him like he wanted him, but then tried talking Nebraska into not kissing him. It was all too much. Nebraska got overwhelmed easily under the slightest bit of confrontation. Too many years of unresolved abuse had left him an anxious mess. He just needed a minute to reevaluate before he ended up running for his life... and then likely losing it.

CHAPTER FOUR

CREE STARED INTO SPACE for much longer than necessary. Nebraska didn't realize it, but Cree had come from even worse abuse than him. Not that it was a competition. He got where he had gone wrong in their conversation. Turning things over in his mind a million times had shown him exactly which wrong words he had used. Cree had made it sound like—despite his claims to the contrary—he didn't, in fact, want Nebraska. Otherwise, he would have just gone for it and then told Nebraska it was okay if he decided to leave one day. Cree only wanted him to be happy.

When Nebraska didn't return, Cree finally went in search of him. He followed the sound of laughter down the hall to the upstairs sitting room. Angel, King, and Nebraska were playing a trivia game. Some of the other guys were gathered around to watch. Cree wasn't surprised. King and Nebraska were both geniuses. It was a sight to behold. He had watched them play this game before. They both knew everything about everything.

"Who's winning?"

Angel turned a laughing gaze Cree's way.

"Are you getting a black eye?"

Cree ignored Angel's question. It took everything he had not to look Nebraska's way.

Finally, Angel gave up and motioned King and Nebraska's way. "They're tied and I'm getting my ass handed to me. So, I've decided to make things interesting."

Nebraska's sexy green gaze turned his way. He looked happy. "If I win, Angel gets to tattoo King with anything of my choosing. If King wins, he gets to choose my first tattoo."

Cree groaned. He hated the idea of anyone marking Nebraska's skin, mostly because of the pain. No pain should ever touch Nebraska again. But it wasn't his skin and Cree had no right to say no. "I can't watch this. I'll be on the patio."

Laughter followed him out the door to the upstairs deck. Cree took a deep breath as the night air washed over him. Archer had chosen a truly beautiful place for them to live. It was nothing but gorgeous trees and water. The place was peaceful. They needed that.

He grabbed a lounge chair and sat. With his gaze locked on the full moon, he pulled out a laced cigar. They were in for the night and Nebraska was happy. Cree could relax and let go for a few. The second he lit up, Archer stepped outside. He filled the lounge next to Cree.

"I thought I'd find you out here."

That was fair. Winter or summer, this was Cree's favorite spot. Cree grunted. He knew Archer wasn't looking for a response.

For a moment, they sat in silence, enjoying the night air, before Archer spoke up again. "You know, I'm still not keen on the idea of Nebraska becoming a guard. That doesn't sound like something he'll enjoy."

"Yeah." Cree had a feeling Archer was right.

"It's okay for him to be here as nothing more than someone for you. That's fine. There are exactly two people in this world I trust: Angel and you. If you say this boy won't sell us out, then cool. You deserve to have something pretty you set on a shelf and spoil. That's what Angel is to me. I would never deny you that. Don't try to make him someone he's not for me, okay?"

Cree nodded. He wasn't sure it had been for Archer. Cree didn't know anymore who he tried to appease. Maybe it was himself. He didn't think he was enough for anyone. Cree was pretty fucked up in the head. Nebraska deserved beautiful things. Cree wasn't beautiful. His soul was black. Tainted. As Nebraska said, fiendish. If Cree hadn't plucked Nebraska from his life, maybe he could've gone to college and been anything. He was amazing. Cree had stolen his life.

"The business we really should discuss is my shit being held hostage in the shipping yard. This isn't the first time we've had this problem, but Journey isn't with us any longer, and I can't roll up in there and kill everyone. We need a hacker. We need someone who can bypass their system and make it look as if all is well, so they'll release my shit."

"I can do that."

Cree's head turned so fast toward the doorway, he nearly injured himself.

Nebraska stood there, twisting his fingers, and looking scared as hell. "I'm good at hacking stuff."

Cree wanted to beg him to shut up before he got himself in too deep, but it was too late. He had Archer's attention.

"You honestly think you could bypass their system? We're not talking high school shit where you change your grades."

Nebraska nodded. "I know. While I used to break into the school system all the time to mark my fees and lunch as paid, because my dad was a shit parent and I would've starved otherwise, I can also break into other things. I hacked the court system and erased my dad's DUIs and got his license back. He never let me learn how to drive, so I couldn't risk him not being able to get groceries. When he actually did, that is."

"Damn. You actually hacked the courts and didn't get caught?"

Nebraska nodded.

Archer looked Cree's way. "If he can do that as a teen with no one backing him, I could keep him safe doing smaller things."

Cree nodded. Again, it was too late, and it wasn't his life. If Nebraska wanted to do this, he couldn't stop him.

"If you point me toward a laptop, I can get you in."

Nebraska's claim had Archer on his feet. "Let's go."

With a smile—like a kid being complimented—Nebraska headed inside with Archer. Cree took a deep drag from his cigar. Once again, he wouldn't watch Nebraska make this choice. However... A smile pulled at the corners of his mouth that had nothing to do with his high. Nebraska couldn't get away from him now. It didn't matter if Cree wasn't good enough for Nebraska. Archer would never let him go. They were stuck.

It took Nebraska less than five minutes to do Archer's task. Archer looked thrilled. King had praised him, and they started talking about setting up a bank account for Nebraska so he could spoil himself. All Nebraska wanted was to be with Cree. He ducked out the first moment he could. Cree was right where Nebraska had left him.

Smoke billowed around him the second he stepped outside. "Holy secondhand high. What are you smoking?"

Cree grabbed his waist and hauled him into his lap. "That was fast."

Nebraska shrugged and cuddled against Cree's huge chest. "I told you I could do it."

Cree took a puff from his cigar and touched Nebraska's chin, urging it up. His lips met Nebraska's. He blew the smoke into Nebraska's mouth. Nebraska automatically inhaled. His head immediately spun. His muscles relaxed. Cree did it again. Nebraska didn't fight. He wanted to let go. His anxiety always ruined things.

"You know Archer won't let you go now, right? What you did tonight made you a prisoner of this life."

Nebraska nodded. "I know."

Cree blew more smoke into Nebraska's mouth. His skin warmed and his tongue loosened. "Maybe I wanted to trap you. Maybe it's you who can't get away now."

If he was bothered, Cree didn't show it. He kept smoking. The smoke billowed around his face, making him look downright evil. "Are you getting inked tonight?"

Nebraska shook his head. "King is currently getting a unicorn tattoo as we speak."

A snort burst from Cree. He snuffed out his cigar and then rearranged Nebraska on his lap, moving Nebraska to straddle him. He held Nebraska's stare, looking high, and turned on. In fact, his erection couldn't be missed between them. "I love having you here with me. That's what I should've said earlier. I didn't mean to make you feel otherwise. You're the best part of my day."

Nebraska tried his ass off, but he couldn't hide his happiness. He scooted even closer to get a better feel of the impressive erection between them. Nebraska was just high enough to be daring. "Does that mean I can kiss you without you complaining?"

A huge grin exploded across Cree's face. "You can do whatever you want to me. I'm game."

Nebraska bit his bottom lip. He hated to bring back any chance Cree might deny him, but he needed to be honest. "I've never been with anyone. Can you teach me?"

Cree snagged the back of Nebraska's head and hauled him forward. Their mouths came together so hard, their teeth bumped. Nebraska moved restlessly against Cree. He had never wanted anything as badly. Before he knew what to expect, Cree's hand found its way inside Nebraska's shorts. A gasp escaped Nebraska as Cree's tight hold surrounded his cock.

"Oh, God." It was such a ridiculously small thing, but Nebraska had been primed for Cree's touch for too long. He leaned his head back and sucked air as Cree's mouth moved to his neck. The competing sensations had him mesmerized.

"You have to look at this tattoo you made me—oops. Sorry."

King's interruption barely registered. He didn't even look toward the door to see if King walked away. Cree never missed a beat in toying with Nebraska's body. "Tell me how you picture this going. I don't want to go farther than you want, and I will if you don't tell me."

Nebraska was too horny and high to play coy. "I want to taste your dick. You have no idea how much I want that."

A pained-sounding groan escaped Cree. "You plan to be the death of me, don't you? With that innocent mouth doing dirty things."

Nebraska didn't care about anything but doing all the things he had pictured doing to Cree. He went straight for the button and zipper on Cree's jeans.

"Fuck."

At Cree's curse, Nebraska froze. "What's wrong?"

A deep, sexy chuckle rumbled from Cree. "That was a good fuck. I don't think anyone has ever been this eager to suck me."

"Oh." Nebraska wondered if he should be embarrassed. But then his fingers encircled Cree's cock, and he forgot to be ashamed. He immediately slithered down Cree's body and licked his crown.

Cree's fingers found Nebraska's hair. Nebraska sucked the tip of Cree's dick. He tried to be gentle. Nebraska didn't want to hurt him. He just wanted a taste.

Cree moaned.

Encouraged, Nebraska kept going. He couldn't take much of Cree without choking. That didn't stop him. He enjoyed the few inches he could reach while still stroking Cree. Nebraska couldn't imagine Cree getting off only by him licking him, so he kept pumping. Maybe a hand job wasn't what Cree wanted, but Nebraska wasn't ready to give up his feast. A hint of salt coated his tongue. Nebraska wanted more.

"Damn, beautiful. You're killing me."

Nebraska lifted his head. "Do you want me to stop?"

A bright smile lit Cree's face. "You really need a lesson in praise. Don't stop."

Nebraska went back to enjoying himself. He decided to ignore anything else Cree said. Nebraska was too turned on and enjoyed himself too much to learn a lesson on praise tonight. He wanted Cree to come in his mouth. The more Nebraska got into it, the more guttural the sounds were coming from Cree. His hips moved, fucking Nebraska's palm and mouth. It was sexy. Nebraska felt powerful. He had Cree under his spell. Wow. It was so much better than he expected. Cree's grip tightened on Nebraska's hair. He didn't really like that, but his irritation wasn't enough to make him stop. Cree's breathing sounded ragged and desperate.

Nebraska sucked a little harder. Pumped faster.

"Oh fuck, baby. I'm about to come. I don't want to come in your mouth."

That was disappointing. Nebraska lifted his head. Cree tugged Nebraska's hair, forcing him to meet his gaze. He took over, jacking off while Nebraska took in every detail. It didn't take long before Cree cried out. Cum hit Nebraska's face. Nebraska automatically closed his eyes so he wouldn't end up blinded. A moan escaped him without thought as the warm liquid hit his cheek. He licked the bit of cum that hit his lips. With his eyes closed, he savored Cree's taste. It was everything he dreamed it would be.

Cree quickly peeled off his shirt and wiped the cum from Nebraska's face. The last thing he wanted was for any more of his jizz to end up in Nebraska's mouth. Nebraska didn't deserve that. He wasn't like Cree. Nebraska didn't know the things Cree had done to survive. He deserved someone better than Cree. Someone clean of sin. Cree would not come in his perfect mouth.

With Nebraska's face clean, Cree tossed his shirt aside and snagged Nebraska. He stood, bringing Nebraska with him. With a twist, he sat Nebraska on the lounge chair with his back to the door.

Cree met King's stare where he stood in the shadows. He had known the guy was there the entire time. Nebraska hadn't stopped when he had noisily stepped out, and some guys just liked to watch. Cree wasn't the type to care. In fact, he needed King to see Nebraska belonged to him.

"My turn."

Cree dropped to his knees and easily set Nebraska's cock free from his workout shorts.

Nebraska turned openly nervous for the first time. He licked his lips and didn't meet Cree's stare head on. "You don't have to do this."

The smile that stretched Cree's lips felt evil. "I don't think you realize how long I've wanted this." Nebraska's gaze finally met his. Cree let him see his lust. "Don't deny me."

Nebraska gave a small nod.

That was all Cree needed. He dropped his head and swallowed Nebraska's cock. "Oh, God. You're way better at this than I am. I can't do that."

Cree didn't acknowledge the ridiculous statement. He had way more practice, and that wasn't a good thing. Cree didn't know how to explain Nebraska's innocence was way better than his debauchery. Nebraska had done something sweet for him because he wanted to and because he cared. Cree was good because he had to be. Not this time. This time, it was because he loved someone. His eyes burned at the thought. Nebraska ran his fingers through Cree's hair and scratched his scalp, as if comforting him while he sucked Nebraska's dick. That had him getting even more emotional. Cree was never in his feelings like this. Being on his knees for Nebraska was different. It was special.

Nebraska got into it, and Cree's mind went quiet. His only focus was bringing Nebraska pleasure. He abused his throat. Cree put every ounce of his talent into licking and sucking. Nebraska was wild beneath him. Everything Nebraska did made him feel more desired than he ever had before. Nebraska made him want to be better. He bobbed faster, following the sounds Nebraska made. Nebraska kept stroking his hair and face. Everything about him was so loving. Cree wanted to give him the world.

Nebraska's cries and moans got more desperate. Cree kept going. A final loud cry caressed his ears. Hot cum filled his mouth. Cree turned his head and spit. He couldn't swallow, not even for Nebraska. Cree had too much PTSD. Too many times he had been purposely made to choke on someone's cum he didn't want. Still, he kind of hated himself in that moment. He wanted to be someone else. Then Nebraska stroked his face and brought his lips to his. The sweetest kiss he ever experienced rocked his soul. He felt worthy, and it sucker punched him harder than he expected.

Cree's arms locked around Nebraska. He held on for dear life as their tongues stroked. This one was his. Archer was right. It was okay for him to have one thing. He would take it.

CHAPTER FIVE

FOR HOURS, THEY HELD each other in bed. Their toes played beneath the covers. Cree kept stroking Nebraska's stomach, making him feel more treasured than he ever had. The moment felt perfect. Each time Cree's lips found his, Nebraska thought he might cry. He had never known this much happiness.

Cree's mouth covered his. This time, things weren't as sweet. Nebraska's body stirred. Cree shifted. His huge body found its way between Nebraska's thighs. Nebraska's body cradled his as they explored each other's mouth. They were a quiet passion. Nebraska didn't know how to explain that. He had just spent so much of his life in panicked turmoil. Cree felt peaceful even when he set Nebraska ablaze. Nebraska didn't know where things were headed this time. Maybe Cree only wanted to hold him. Nebraska really wanted to get fucked, but he was too shy to say that. His earlier high was gone, so too was his bravery.

Cree shifted positions again. This time, he trapped Nebraska between his thighs and lowered his weight. When their bodies met, so did their erections. Nebraska gasped at the sensation. Cree's hips rolled. The friction made him want to beg. Cree's phone chirped. They froze.

"Fuck." Cree moved away to grab his phone. Nebraska knew he couldn't ignore it. It was his job to be at Archer's beck and call. "Goddamn it. Archer needs me to handle something."

Nebraska wanted to groan and beg him to stay. He equally wanted to know what Archer could possibly need handled at two in the morning. Nebraska knew better than to say any of that. He probably didn't want to know.

"Okay. Be careful."

Cree leaned in one more time and captured Nebraska's lips. They clung for a second before Cree moved away to dress. Nebraska listened to him gathering his things in the dark. Even though his body still burned for Cree, it was strangely sweet the way Cree didn't turn on the light to dress, as if he didn't want to bother Nebraska.

"Get some sleep."

"Okay."

Cree stepped out and Nebraska caught sight of King in the hall. Voices rumbled through the door after Cree closed it, but Nebraska couldn't make out what was said. He tried closing his eyes, willing himself to sleep. His mind raced too fast. Happiness kept him from relaxing. An hour into waiting for Cree's return, Nebraska threw in the towel. He climbed from bed and found some pajama pants. King had sleeping pills. That guy had everything, including an obvious addiction. That bothered Nebraska a little. He genuinely liked King. Nebraska's dad had been an addict. It was an ugly thing Nebraska wanted to leave behind. But King didn't act like his father had and Nebraska knew from experience he couldn't change anyone.

Nebraska padded across the hall. King's light was on. Since he had left with Cree, Nebraska opened the door without knocking. He froze. So too did King, who had very much not left with Cree. King was shirtless. He had on fishnet stockings and a schoolgirl type plaid skirt that barely covered his ass.

Nebraska jumped inside the room and closed the door behind him before anyone else came along and saw. "Oh, my God. I'm so sorry. I thought you left with Cree, and I just wanted to grab a sleeping pill. You said I could anytime I needed."

King looked like a deer caught in headlights. "Please don't tell."

Nebraska's shoulders relaxed. "I would never do that, and damn, look at you. You look amazing."

He really did. His thick, muscular thighs looked surprisingly sexy in fishnets.

A small smile touched King's lips. He still looked uncomfortable. "You can grab whatever you need. You know where I keep everything."

Instead of heading for King's stash, Nebraska moved to the bed and sat. He was fascinated. "Do you do makeup too or just clothes?"

King didn't answer. "We're short-handed right now, so we're doing most things alone rather than in pairs, like we used to do. That's why I'm not with Cree."

Nebraska stood. He could just forget this. That was obviously what King wanted. "It's okay. You're allowed to have secrets. If you ever decide you want to talk, though, I'm here. Judgment free. Just so you know." Nebraska headed for King's stash.

"I do the makeup too. But it's already late and I can't really go anywhere with Cree gone, so there's no point. I just wanted... something tonight."

Nebraska nodded. He decided to jump in with both feet since King opened the line of communication. "I'm here, and I'm not the least bit tired. If you want to do your makeup and model outfits, I'd love to watch."

A bright smile lit King's face. "Okay."

Nebraska moved back to the bed and sat cross-legged. King got started. He chattered happily as he moved around the room. Nebraska couldn't stop smiling. King had always made him feel welcome and accepted, while most everyone else had made him feel like a problem to be solved. Nebraska wanted to give back that same gift to King. Plus, he truly was interested in this side of King. He felt like someone's friend. It had been a long time since he felt that way. Nebraska didn't want the feeling to end.

Cree resented every second of having to take care of business in the middle of the night. By the time he made it back home, he felt growly, and he wanted to get back in bed with Nebraska. He hadn't stopped thinking about leaving his baby behind, warm and hard. Goddamn. He was already addicted.

Unfortunately, as he opened the bedroom door, the room was already lit with the morning light and Nebraska wasn't in bed. Cree checked the bathroom. He wasn't there. Cree had come through the kitchen as he came inside the house, so he knew Nebraska wasn't there. He stepped back into the hall. King's bedroom door opened, and Nebraska stepped out. He was only wearing pajama pants and looked every bit as surprised to see Cree as Cree was to see him coming out of King's room.

Nebraska's face lit, as if a light switch had been thrown inside him. "Hey. I didn't know you were home." He held up a pill bottle. "I gave up on sleeping to beg King for some sleeping pills. Until tonight, I hadn't realized how much I can't sleep when you're not here."

The pressure in Cree's chest eased. He didn't honestly think he had a reason to be jealous, but he was. Maybe King's presence outside earlier had been more about watching Nebraska than he realized. Cree was ridiculously obsessed with Nebraska. It made sense someone else could be too. "You don't need those. I'm here now." Cree closed the distance between them and plucked Nebraska off his feet. He tossed Nebraska over his shoulder and headed for bed. The moment they were shut away inside their bedroom, Cree tossed Nebraska on the bed. He followed him down. Nebraska tugged at Cree's clothes. Their kiss only broke each time an article of clothing disappeared. Before long, Cree had Nebraska back where he wanted him: pinned beneath him with their dicks rubbing against each other. He recognized his kiss was rougher than he wanted. Possessiveness drove him. He felt like he needed to mark his territory.

Cree reached between their bodies and grabbed their cocks. He held them together as he pumped. Nebraska moaned and fought for air beneath him. Cree didn't let up. He needed Nebraska to know where he belonged. To whom he belonged. Nebraska's short nails dug into Cree's shoulders. He couldn't tell if Nebraska meant to pull him closer or push him away.

That knowledge was like ice water in the face. He froze. His gaze found Nebraska's. Panic seized his chest. Sometimes, he scared himself. How could he expect Nebraska to not be afraid? He didn't deserve him.

"Don't stop."

Nebraska's breathless whisper broke through the terror that seized him. His muscles relaxed. His mouth found Nebraska's. This time, he moved slower. Their encounter turned to lovemaking. He cherished Nebraska. When Nebraska blew beneath him, something melted inside Cree. He couldn't stop kissing Nebraska, even as an intense orgasm hit, leveling him. Cree moaned around Nebraska's tongue as he pumped out every drop of cum. He would try harder to be better. That was what Nebraska deserved.

CHAPTER SIX

NEBRASKA SPENT HIS NIGHTS beneath Cree, begging for release. Each time Cree left him behind to work, he spent his free time with King. Nebraska enjoyed their time together. He honestly thought of King as his best friend. After two months of talking to King about everything under the sun, and Cree still not initiating penetrative sex, Nebraska fought the urge to ask King's opinion. In theory, he knew he should be able to talk to Cree. But Nebraska had become a bit self-conscious about it since he was used to coming up short. He couldn't understand why Cree wasn't interested. Unless he just wasn't interested in sex with Nebraska. He felt very naïve and completely inadequate. Nebraska thought about it more than might be healthy.

Nebraska chewed the side of his nail while he watched King do his make-up. King would go out tonight and Nebraska was still trapped with his spiraling thoughts. He wanted to be wanted. Despite the nightly orgasms, Nebraska wasn't sure what was real.

"Can I talk to you about something uncomfortably personal?"

King met his stare in the mirror. A smile lit his face. "Since you know all my deepest darkest, it's probably fair."

Nebraska took a breath and then lost his courage. "What do you do at this club?"

King shrugged. "I like to watch." He met Nebraska's gaze again. "You understand?"

Nebraska nodded. King had watched him with Cree. He got it. Unfortunately, he wasn't sure what it said about him that he had enjoyed it too. Maybe that was why Cree didn't want more.

"Now, do you want to tell me what you really wanted to talk about? You know way too much about me to be embarrassed."

"Do you have any idea why Cree doesn't want sex with me?" The question burst from Nebraska, sounding as desperate as he felt.

King turned in his chair. "The moans coming from your rooms would say otherwise."

Nebraska blushed hot. "I mean, like he doesn't..." Nebraska couldn't say the words.

King's eyebrows rose. "I can't help if you don't tell me the whole of it."

Damn. Nebraska couldn't stop blushing. "I mean, um. This is torture. He doesn't... like there's no penetration." Nebraska wanted to die. He had never been more embarrassed.

"Oh." King stood and moved to sit on the bed with Nebraska. "Penetration doesn't equal sex. Sex looks different for everyone. But there might be a lot of different reasons and all I can do is speculate. Some people don't like that. Others find it downright gross. Cree may be scared to hurt you. My guess is, though, it's likely the way we were raised."

After King's speech, Nebraska's embarrassment vanished. It was replaced with curiosity. "What do you mean?"

For a moment, King watched him with a blank stare. Finally, he shook his head slightly, as if breaking a trance. "Has Cree never talked to you about how we were raised?"

Nebraska shrugged. "He's made a few off-hand comments that lead me to believe his past isn't happy, so I don't ask. It's not like I want to talk about my past either."

King nodded. "I understand, but if you want to understand Cree, you should know."

"Okay."

King's chest expanded as he took a deep breath. "Years ago, there used to be this group of men who bought kids from orphanages around the country."

"Bought?"

King nodded. "It was a big business for under-funded orphanages. Anyhow, they needed a certain type. Boys who were tall or muscular for their age. Kids they could twist into monsters."

"Why?" Nebraska was horrified and fascinated.

"To make us into killers and then sell our services to people like Archer."

"So Archer actually owns Cree? Like owns, owns? Like a slave?"

King shook his head. "Archer is younger than Cree. He went through the program after Cree. No, Cree was bought by Archer's first husband. Except he wanted more than a trained assassin at his beck and call. He kept Cree as more of a sex slave. That didn't end until Archer came to live with him. Archer was younger, more calculating, and not above seducing a powerful man to take his spot. Cree serves Archer out of loyalty and gratitude. Archer saved him from a life on his knees. Can you imagine what you would do for someone who saved you from basically being sexually assaulted every day? Can you imagine what his mind must be like when it comes to sexual matters? It's not like any of us get counseling. What would we tell a shrink? Hey, I kill people and grown men used to beat me and pass me around like a two-dollar whore at a frat party."

Cold settled into Nebraska's bones. He hated all of this for Cree and King. "Thank you for telling me. I'm sorry you went through that."

King shrugged. "We all have our crosses, and we all deal with it in our way." King motioned toward himself. "This is how I cope. Cree kills people. You do what you gotta do."

Nebraska nodded. A door slammed in the hallway. Nebraska scrambled from the bed. "Have fun tonight," he called over his shoulder as he slipped from the room.

Cree stood in the hallway, looking pissed. "Why in the fuck are you always in King's bedroom when I get home?"

Nebraska didn't answer. He closed the distance between them, wrapped his arms around Cree, and held on. After a moment, he felt Cree relax.

He stroked Nebraska's hair. "What's wrong?"

Nebraska shook his head. "Nothing. I just missed you and want to hold you." His feet left the floor as Cree lifted Nebraska into his arms. Nebraska wrapped his legs around Cree, hanging on like a kid as Cree carried him to their bedroom. "I brought you dinner."

Nebraska smiled like an idiot. "Did you? Take me to bed, then, and I'll enjoy my meal."

Cree snorted. "It's pizza. I want you to get some actual food in your belly. Also, FYI, I'd never talk to you like that. You're my baby. You deserve respect."

Nebraska couldn't stop smiling. "What if I want to be disrespected?"

Cree set him on the settee and pointed to a nearby pizza box. "Eat."

Since it seemed important to Cree, Nebraska opened the box. "Oooh. It's extra cheesy." He happily chose a piece and took a bite. "Mmm. So good." Cree looked appeased. That was all that mattered to Nebraska. He only wanted Cree's happiness. That would always be his top priority.

For months, Cree had been coming home, finding Nebraska with King. He was more than a little pissed off about it. If anything was going on between the two, Nebraska's hunger for Cree hadn't lessened. They definitely had a healthy sex life. In fact, the extra workout had Cree in damn good shape.

As always, the longer he sat with Nebraska, the more he relaxed. Nebraska was so adorable, and he was obviously happy to be with Cree. Cree let it go. He waited until Nebraska finished his slice before he grabbed the gift bag he had hidden behind the settee. Cree handed it to Nebraska.

"Here."

Nebraska lit like a kid on Christmas. "You bought me a gift?"

Cree shrugged and moved the pizza box so he could sit next to Nebraska. He would have to remember to buy things for Nebraska more often. It was nice making him happy. "I think this is long overdue."

Nebraska dug into the bag, tossing tissue paper with abandon. "It's a phone." He looked stunned. Tears filled his eyes. "You're trusting me with a phone?"

Cree realized he should have done this much sooner. By giving Nebraska no way to view the outside world, he had made him feel more like a prisoner. "Of course. I'm not holding you hostage. Plus, it occurred to me tonight that you didn't have a way to reach me when I'm gone. If you need anything, you need to have a way to let me know." Plus, it had GPS tracking, so Cree could always find him.

Nebraska set the phone aside and moved to straddle Cree. "This is amazing. Thank you."

Cree's arms automatically encircled Nebraska. "You're amazing. I don't think I say that or show you enough."

Nebraska shook his head. "Never doubt yourself with me. You've given me the best life I've ever had."

That was depressing. A fucking phone gave Nebraska the best life he ever had. He was a piece of shit for being surly lately. Nebraska definitely deserved better than him. Cree couldn't make Nebraska happy enough to suit his heart.

"I love you."

Nebraska blinked, as if that was the last thing he ever expected Cree to say. His eyes filled with tears again. He sniffed. "I love you too."

Cree knew that. He hadn't thought he needed the words, though. Now that Nebraska had said them, Cree already wanted to hear them again. "I love you."

A bright smile lit Nebraska's face even as his eyes shone bright with tears. "I love you too."

"What do you want to drink? It's really important to me that you eat dinner."

"You know what I like."

Cree brushed his lips across Nebraska's mouth and then stood. He set Nebraska on the spot he had vacated and handed him the pizza box. "Eat. I'll be right back."

Nebraska dutifully grabbed another slice. Cree dashed out to the kitchen. He snagged a grape soda from the fridge and headed back upstairs. King's bedroom door opened and closed just as quickly, as if King had spotted him and changed his mind. Cree shook his head. Something was going on, but damned if he could put his finger on it. The secretiveness bothered him again until he opened the door to find Nebraska eating pizza with one hand while playing with his phone with the other.

He looked up as Cree came through the door. "You already have everyone's number programmed."

"I wanted to make sure you have options in case anything ever happens."

"That's so sweet."

It wasn't. They lived a dangerous life. He had killed once for Nebraska. Cree wouldn't hesitate to do it again. His mind shifted back to King. He hoped that one wasn't the next.

Nebraska made room for Cree to sit. "We need a picture so I can set my background image."

Cree kissed Nebraska's cheek. Nebraska captured the moment. He stared at the image for a few seconds. "Let's get another one. I want to see your gorgeous eyes."

This time, Nebraska quickly turned his head and kissed Cree's cheek as he took the picture. He smiled as he stared at the image. Nebraska turned the phone Cree's way. "Look at you."

Cree blinked as he stared at the photo. He didn't even look like himself. A bright smile had exploded across his face the moment Nebraska had kissed him. He had never seen himself so happy. It was like looking at a stranger. Not for the first time, it hit Cree how far he would go to keep this. He had never been a sane man. Cree was even less so when he thought about losing Nebraska. He would never let that happen. They were to the grave.

Cree always made Nebraska so happy he couldn't contain it. Each time he thought

Cree couldn't get better, he did shit like give him a phone, proving this was real. He believed enough in their relationship to trust Nebraska with a way to reach the outside world. It was a stupid little thing, but it made Nebraska feel like this was forever. The happiness in his chest over Cree admitting he loved him had nowhere to go. He was restless. Nebraska needed to do something before he burst.

"Can we go somewhere?"

Cree looked thoughtful. "What did you have in mind?"

Nebraska honestly didn't know. He was just restless. An idea hit. "King is always telling me about this club he goes to."

"Oh, lord. I can't imagine."

A smile snapped to Nebraska's lips. "I don't want to go there." He bit his lip, wondering if he would get shot down. Finally, he decided to just give it a shot. "But I'd really love to go somewhere and dance with you."

Cree looked thoughtful for a moment. He stood, forcing Nebraska to drop his feet to the floor. "I have an idea. Let's go."

Nebraska practically danced down the stairs, following Cree. They got their shoes and headed for the garage. As Cree drove, Nebraska fought the urge to bounce in his seat. To his surprise, Cree didn't head toward town. He drove them to a quiet beach. Nebraska looked Cree's way when he parked.

Cree flashed him a smile and found a playlist on his phone to blast through the speakers. He opened the door. "Come on."

Nebraska slipped from the SUV and followed Cree to the back of the vehicle. Cree opened the back hatch and let the music pour out. A bright smile snapped to Nebraska's lips as Cree towed him into his arms. Cree sang to Nebraska as they moved with the music. Nebraska closed his eyes and pressed his ear to Cree's chest. They weren't just loving words. Nebraska knew Cree loved him. He felt it in every action. Every kindness. Nebraska truly believed he saw a side of Cree that Cree reserved solely for him. Never in his life had he felt special. He mattered to Cree.

The first song ended. Cree lifted him from the ground and set him inside the back of the Tahoe. "I need to say something. I don't like you spending so much time with King. You belong to me."

That irritated Nebraska a little. He had spent too much time with no friends because of his dad. "I don't want another father. King is only a friend. You're the one I love. You're the only one for me."

Cree didn't look reassured.

Nebraska couldn't stand the tension in the air. He stroked Cree's stomach and lured him closer. His gaze never wavered from Cree's. "I ache for the moments when I have you to myself. Can I just enjoy this moment with you?"

Cree shook his head, as if physically trying to shake off his mood. A smile tugged at his lips. He dragged Nebraska closer, finding his way between Nebraska's thighs. "You're the greatest thing that's ever happened to me." He brought Nebraska's hand to shape his erection through his pants. "I ache for you too."

Power surged through Nebraska. "I can help with that." He slid Cree's zipper down while holding his stare. A thrill ran through him at the idea of having Cree in a place where anyone could catch them at any time. Each day, he learned something new about himself. He would make love to Cree anywhere. As long as they had each other, everything else would be fine.

CHAPTER SEVEN

THE DAY OF NEBRASKA'S twentieth birthday, he woke up alone. For a moment, he blinked in confusion, wondering if he had slept through Cree telling him goodbye. The empty spot beside him hurt for some reason he couldn't pinpoint. Maybe because this day had never been special for him and today looked to be no different. In fact, Nebraska always suffered the absolute worst luck and hardships on his birthday. In a small secret way, he had hoped this first one with Cree would be different.

After a shower and eating alone, Nebraska headed outside. The wind had a bite to it, signaling the rapidly approaching winter. He walked the well-worn path to the huge pond nearby. It was a beautiful spot and one of the few places he felt free to roam. He headed toward the nearest bench to the water where he always sat. King was already there, staring at nothing. Nebraska didn't think he even heard his approach.

Since all the guys had itchy trigger fingers, he announced his presence before he startled King. "Hey. I didn't expect to find you here."

King blinked and looked his way. "Oh. Hey." He scooted over, making room for

Nebraska. "Why aren't you wearing a coat?"

"I don't have one."

"You don't have one?"

Nebraska shrugged. He didn't want to talk about how he had fled his home state with nothing but a backpack of clothes. Everything he owned now was at the mercy of others.

King stood and peeled off his coat. "Take mine."

Nebraska geared up to protest, but King cut him off before he started. "I'm wearing long sleeves and have over a hundred pounds on you. Trust me, I get overheated easily."

With a nod, Nebraska accepted the coat. It was nice and toasty as he slipped his arms inside. It also swallowed him whole.

King reclaimed his seat. "What drove you out here with no jacket?"

Nebraska shrugged again. He didn't want to admit it was his birthday, and he was sad. "Bored, I guess. Why are you sitting out here alone?"

"I'm always alone."

King said the words to the water, so Nebraska didn't get a look at his face. He understood King meant he was always emotionally alone. They spent too much time together for King to mean the words literally. "What would cheer you up?"

A smile flashed his way. "Do you ever worry about yourself, or do you only care about other people?"

Nebraska shoved his hands between his knees so he wouldn't fidget and give away how much that question bothered him. He wasn't selfless. Nebraska wanted things. He had just given up. Life had beaten him. He didn't have the energy to fight for anything. So, he chose another path. "I care about you."

King looked away again. "You probably shouldn't. I don't think Cree likes that we're friends. He's been kind of an asshole to me lately."

That might have been true, but Nebraska had decided not to let that deter him. He had given up everything, even a fucking coat, to be with Cree. Cree could allow him one friend, and King needed him. "He hasn't told me we can't be friends."

A wry smile passed over King's lips. "Give it time."

Nebraska refused to be sad anymore. "Well, that day isn't today, so what should we do?"

"Archer almost caught me leaving last night. Now I don't feel like I can dress how I want. It was too close of a call."

"Get a hotel room and dress there before you go out. Problem solved."

King's gaze swung his way. For the first time, Nebraska saw how unhappy he was. "I don't want to be this way."

Nebraska took his hand. "Why? You're beautiful just the way you are." He kissed

King's hand. "How about this? What if I go with you?"

King snorted. "I'm not taking you to my club. That's not a place for you."

Nebraska curled his nose. "I don't mean there. Cree would die. I meant, grab your stuff and I'll go to the hotel with you. We could grab some food and we could even find me an outfit and I'll dress up with you. It's not the club, but if you start feeling better, you can head over for a couple of hours, and I'll hang out at the hotel. I can watch a movie and eat snacks. That's all I do here, and Cree is gone. I don't know where or when he's coming back. That's pretty typical."

"You sounded a little bitter right then."

A sardonic smile pulled at Nebraska's lips. He still didn't want to admit it was his birthday. "Let's focus on a problem we can solve."

King didn't look mollified, but—thankfully—he let it go. "Okay. Let's grab my stuff and head out. If nothing else, we can make your birthday fun."

A bright smile exploded across Nebraska's face. "Shut up. You remembered?"

King stood. "Of course. You're my best friend. How could I forget?"

The statement hit harder than Nebraska expected. Cree hadn't noticed. In fact, he couldn't recall if Cree had ever asked about the date of his birthday. It seemed he was pretty forgettable to the person he loved the most. That tracked.

Cree spent the entire day going from store to store, buying everything he could think of to get for the perfect birthday party. By the time he got home, he wanted to pat himself on the back for how perfect things would be. He was a tad surprised Nebraska hadn't called or texted, demanding to know why he had sneaked away without saying goodbye. On his birthday, no less. Once again, Nebraska was nowhere to be found. This time, he went straight to King's bedroom. He didn't knock. Cree burst in, half expecting to find them in bed. The room was empty.

It wasn't like he hadn't mentioned how uncomfortable he was with how close they were. Now they were missing. His temper spiked so hard and fast, his head pounded. Cree stamped down the stairs. He found Angel on the couch, reading a book.

"Have you seen Nebraska?"

Angel flipped his page without looking Cree's way. "He went to run errands with King."

Cree tried taking a breath, but there was a knot in his gut that wouldn't budge. "How long ago was that?"

Angel shrugged. "After breakfast."

Cree saw red. He ran his hand through his hair and dug out his phone. It was nearly seven. There was nothing King could take Nebraska to do that should last that long. He pulled up the GPS tracking app linked to Nebraska's phone. It pinged at an address in town. Cree searched the address. It was a hotel.

"That mother—" Cree headed for the garage without looking back. He didn't think. Cree couldn't. Everything was a black cloud of rage he couldn't see past. He drove twice the speed limit and tore into the parking lot on nearly two wheels. Thankfully, the guy at the front desk wasn't above taking bribes. Cree had their room number in under ten minutes. Still, each one felt like an eternity. As he exited the elevator on their floor, he pulled his gun from its holster. King was dead. Cree wouldn't endure this betrayal. Nothing mattered anymore except Nebraska. Losing him meant losing the last of his sanity.

Cree didn't knock. He wouldn't give them a chance to scramble. Cree lifted his foot and kicked the door open with more force than necessary. It came halfway off its hinges.

Nebraska sat on the hotel bed with a hamburger lifted halfway to his mouth. His eyes were wide. The moment he caught sight of Cree's gun, his burger dropped into the food container on the bed. Nebraska scrambled away and crouched between the mattress and the wall, looking terrified.

"Where is he?"

Nebraska shook like a leaf. His eyes never left the gun. Cree felt zero remorse. He was glad he was scared. Nebraska needed a healthy dose of reality. He had signed King's death warrant.

Cree's gaze scanned the room. The beds were perfectly made. A kid's movie played on the TV. King wasn't in sight. Cree checked the bathroom and closet. There was no way to get under the bed.

"Where is he?"

Nebraska shook his head. "Not here. He went out with friends."

"Get your shit."

With wide eyes, Nebraska shook his head again. "I don't have anything other than my dinner. I only planned to watch a movie."

"Don't give me that bullshit. You have a fucking TV at home."

He closed the lid of Nebraska's food container and picked it up. "Let's go."

Slowly, Nebraska came to his feet. He headed for the door, wringing his hands. They didn't talk as they made their way back to the SUV. Nebraska climbed into the passenger seat.

Cree passed him the food as he climbed behind the wheel. On the way home, Cree didn't say a word. He was too furious. Nebraska held his silence while keeping his hands clasped so tightly, his knuckles were white.

When they got home, Nebraska walked inside ahead of him. Thankfully, no one was around. Dutifully, Nebraska headed upstairs and into their bedroom. He froze as he stepped inside the room. Balloons were everywhere. Flowers sat by the bed. A cake and ice cream waited. The latter had probably melted. Brightly wrapped presents waited on the bed.

Cree nudged him along and followed him inside before slamming the door. He locked it. "Happy fucking birthday." Cree headed for the settee and sat. His rage had him scared of himself. Even he didn't know what he would do, but he knew it wouldn't be good.

Nebraska followed a little slower. He sat on the settee and stared at the cake. "This looks nice."

"Eat it, then."

Nebraska didn't respond right away. "I'm not hungry anymore."

Cree's eye twitched. "Then go take a fucking shower. I don't want his stink on you."

"No one's stink is on me." Nebraska said the words, sounding small.

It did nothing to quell Cree's anger. He snatched Nebraska's food from him and tossed it on top of the cake, uncaring if it was ruined. "I said go take a fucking shower."

Nebraska stood and headed for the bathroom without looking back. Cree listened to the water fire to life. His knee bobbed with nowhere for his fury to go. He had killed many people. Never had he wanted anyone dead as badly as he wanted to see King bleed. That motherfucker was in the wind. Cree would find him soon enough. Until then, Nebraska was the only outlet he had for the vengeance in his heart.

By the time Nebraska stepped from the bathroom, wearing nothing but a towel, Cree had zero fucks to give. Nebraska's eyes and nose were red, as if he had been crying. All Cree could think was *good*. He had demolished Cree. The least he could do was shed a tear.

Cree stood. Nebraska was clean now and Cree could only punish him one way: by showing him what he had lost.

Nebraska's insides shook. He had never feared Cree. He did now. Cree had the same look his father always had before he hurt Nebraska. Nebraska knew the physical pain would join the mental torture soon. He smelled the violence in the air.

His face turned up as Cree came to stand over him. Hurt and rage flashed in Cree's eyes. Nebraska fought the urge to apologize and explain. He couldn't reveal King's secrets and anything he said would fall on deaf ears. They were too far gone. He didn't understand why Cree trusted him so little. Why couldn't he see he was everything to Nebraska?

Cree bent as if to kiss him and obviously changed his mind at the last second. Instead, he buried his face against Nebraska's neck.

"I won't kiss the lips that obviously belong to him." He said the words against Nebraska's skin before opening his mouth and sucking Nebraska's neck.

Nebraska's knees weakened. A sob rose in Nebraska's throat. He loved Cree more than life. Nebraska didn't know how to fix this. He couldn't go back to being alone. When his knees nearly gave out, Cree clasped a tight arm around him. He headed for the bed. With a swipe, Cree sent Nebraska's presents flying. The room spun. Nebraska found himself with no towel and face down on the mattress. The rough treatment had made his face bounce against the mattress. He knew the exact moment his nose started bleeding. Nebraska did nothing to stop it. He was too deep in his shock.

Cree didn't speak. He bit a path down Nebraska's spine. Nebraska hid his face. He locked his back teeth to keep them from chattering.

Cree moved away for a moment. Nebraska was too scared to move or look. Before he had time to wonder what would happen next, cool moisture swept his ass crack. Cree's fingers toyed with his hole.

Despite everything, Nebraska was hard. He couldn't help it. His body knew it was Cree. Cree stretched him. He wasn't gentle. Before Nebraska knew what to expect, Cree impaled him. A pained cry tore from his throat. It was so much worse than he anticipated. Cree didn't slow. The longer he pumped inside Nebraska, the number Nebraska felt. Part of him still knew he could tell Cree to stop and he would. Then again, Nebraska also felt like he couldn't ask Cree to stop. He felt this was the only way he could make things better. Tears silently streamed, soaking the comforter along with his blood. Nebraska stayed still and wondered why he had wanted this. Then the clearest reality settled in and every ounce of will left Nebraska. This was punishment. That was why Cree had never done this before. He saw penetration as something only used to humiliate and discipline. Something broke inside Nebraska. He no longer felt a thing. Cree's hatred choked him. He had never felt as broken.

Even as Cree pulled out and splashed cum across his back, Nebraska felt nothing.

Cree disappeared and then reappeared with a warm washcloth. In a detached way, he knew—under any other circumstances—he would have been humiliated by the way Cree wiped his ass. Nebraska had gone limp. He had nothing left. Cree had shattered him. Thankfully, Cree didn't try to pleasure him. Nebraska knew he could, and he hated that. Cree rearranged Nebraska on the bed and covered him. After turning off the lights, he climbed in next to Nebraska and roughly dragged Nebraska into his hold.

With his back against Cree's chest, Nebraska stared into the dark. Several times, Cree kissed his neck. Nebraska didn't think he even blinked. The shock and heartache had leveled him. Time passed with no meaning. When Cree's breathing deepened, Nebraska eased away. In the dark, he silently dressed. Everything hurt. He prayed Cree didn't wake. Nebraska couldn't fight. He was alive, but dead. Cree had finally given what he wanted, and it had been in cruelty.

Thankfully, Nebraska made it out of the bedroom without Cree stopping him. When he got downstairs, he found Angel on the couch. He wanted to walk right by and out the door. Unfortunately, he wasn't completely dumb. He didn't know how to drive. Nebraska didn't even own a coat. It was in the thirties outside and they were miles from anywhere.

"Please help."

Angel looked up from his book and froze. Nebraska didn't know how he looked, but he imagined he was a mess. Angel was a huge tattoo-covered bear. He couldn't imagine Angel being shocked by much, but he shot to his feet when he saw Nebraska. The concern on Angel's face broke through to him, stealing the shock. Nebraska burst into tears.

"Holy shit. What happened?"

Nebraska didn't know where to start. He shook his head. "I don't know where to go. I can't stay here." Nebraska shook so hard, his teeth chattered.

"Okay. It's alright. Come on." Angel led Nebraska into the mudroom and helped him into his shoes. He grabbed a thick coat and wrapped Nebraska inside. In a matter of minutes, he found himself in the passenger seat of a truck he had never been in. They rode in silence. In less than ten minutes, Angel pulled into a partially hidden driveway. It felt like they went miles before coming to a cabin in the woods. The place was dark.

Angel slipped from the truck. "Come on. You can stay here. This used to belong to one of Archer's employees, but it's been vacant for a while. Still, it should have everything you need. I'll get some groceries and whatnot delivered ASAP."

Nebraska stood by the truck. He didn't move toward the cabin. "Please don't tell Cree where I am. I'm not—" Nebraska didn't know what he meant to say. He wasn't safe. Maybe. He didn't know. His brain didn't work anymore.

"I won't. I promise."

Nebraska finally headed toward the door.

Angel unlocked it and let Nebraska inside. He turned on the lights. It was nice. The place definitely smelled like it had been empty for a while, but it was actually pretty gorgeous. Whoever had lived there had either died or left everything behind. It looked exactly like someone walked away one day and didn't look back.

"Here." He pushed a cellphone Nebraska's way. "Keep this. I have a second phone I keep hidden in case we're ever forced to flee. You can find that number under 'second phone.' Text me if you need anything."

Nebraska nodded, feeling numb. Within minutes, he was alone. The moment the silence settled into his soul; the real tears began. He knew nothing would ever be right again.

Cree came awake with a start. He didn't know if it was the empty spot beside him or the footsteps in the hall. Either way, his heart immediately climbed into his throat. Panic struck. His gaze shot around the room.

"Nebraska?"

No response came.

Cree shot from the bed and turned on the lights. The place felt devoid of life and joy. Then he heard King's voice outside and rage filled him. If they were together again, they were both dead. He snatched up his pants and jerked them on before grabbing his gun. Cree stuffed it in the back of his pants as he yanked open the door.

Angel and King froze. Nebraska was nowhere in sight.

Cree sprang. "You motherfucker. What have you done with Nebraska?"

Cree's back hit the wall so hard and fast, his head bounced, and stars popped in the corners of his eyes. King's thick forearm leaned on Cree's windpipe, cutting off his air. His eyes flashed like a man who had passed insanity.

"Don't come at me unless you're prepared to reap the consequences. I'm not the hundred-and-twenty-pound twink that you toss around and bully."

"You're dead." The words sounded hoarse under the pressure of being choked.

King snorted. "Insanity trumps anger every fucking time and I'm a crazy motherfucker who can't wait to take you apart. What kind of son of a bitch harms the man who loves him more than life only because he was trying to be a good friend? As far as I'm concerned, you're better off dead."

"Break it up. What the fuck is going on up here?"

King didn't back away immediately at Archer's shout. He held Cree's stare. His expression screamed Cree had better not sleep or he would get his throat slit. Finally, he backed away.

His gaze never wavered from Cree. "Ask this bastard. He's the one who thinks he has all the answers and enjoys breaking boys."

Cree couldn't breathe and it had nothing to do with King nearly choking him to death. Something clicked. He turned away and headed for his room.

Archer grabbed his shoulder. "Hold up. We're not finished here."

Cree pulled the gun from his waistband. He had it held to Archer's temple before he knew what he had done. "Go away from me."

Archer held his stare. He didn't look scared. "Pull the trigger, then."

Fucking bastard. Cree lowered the gun and headed inside his room. He slammed the door closed and locked it behind him. Cree couldn't talk to anyone. He couldn't have anyone looking at him. The pieces of his shattered heart felt like they rattled inside his chest.

Too late, Cree realized he might be wrong. There was something about the way King looked at him. Cree had seen that craziness in the mirror. It was helpless rage in a situation out of their control.

Then there was the blood. There had been so much blood after he fucked Nebraska. He feared he might have done some internal damage. Nebraska was somewhere either hiding from him or being kept safe from him. Probably both. Cree shook uncontrollably. He fought the urge to put the gun to his head. Too many times, he had almost lost this battle. The gun rose. The cold barrel pressed against his temple. Everything he owned would become Nebraska's and everyone would be better for it. His gaze focused on something on the floor. It was one of Nebraska's gifts. His knees gave out. Cree's back slid down the door until he landed with a thump on his ass. Everything was gone. It was his fault. Nothing would ever be the same.

CHAPTER EIGHT

WEEKS PASSED. THE SILENCE and solitude of the cabin allowed an ounce of peace to settle into Nebraska's soul. He spent his days digging through all the amazing items inside the cabin. There was a ton of stuff obviously from other countries. Nebraska searched some pieces online so he could read the lore behind them. He realized how big the world was and how little he had seen.

Archer had stopped by a few times, asking for help with odd online jobs. Nebraska always helped. Money showed up in his account afterward. They never talked about Cree. The first time he had come, Nebraska had nearly broken down again. But Archer came and went with no open judgment and Cree never showed up at his door afterward. Eventually, he accepted Archer kept his secret. He had suffered his first Crohn's flareup all alone since meeting Cree. Thankfully, Angel had shown him how to get his meds delivered. There was that. He felt like a real adult now.

Oddly, Nebraska hadn't thought about Cree day and night like he expected. He had expected the loss to gnaw a hole in his gut. Instead, his mind always shied away from the memories, as if protecting itself. The worst was Christmas. Another holiday came and went in silence. He lost another calendar year to emptiness.

Archer and Angel were the only ones who came around. Archer came with work. Angel brought food, toiletries, and clothing. Neither ever stayed long. Conversation was stilted, and Nebraska preferred the silence. The silence didn't see him. He was too broken for anyone else.

Several times, he had pulled out Angel's phone and thought about texting King. Then he would see King's name and go cold. It wasn't King's fault. Nebraska hoped he was okay, but still, Nebraska had nothing to give. He didn't want to hear anyone's voice. Reality hurt too much.

Smoke billowed around Cree's head. It was so cold, he could see his breath. Yet Cree didn't move from his spot on the deck. Everywhere he looked, he still saw Nebraska. Yet he couldn't stop gravitating toward the places where they spent most of their time. They had made love that first time on this lounge. Things had been beautiful then. Cree hadn't yet let the past ruin his future. There were so many things he should have told Nebraska. His actions still wouldn't be forgiven, but maybe Nebraska could find some peace in knowing Cree was just a hopeless head case. Irredeemable. Too fucked up to love him right.

He no longer spoke to anyone. Archer had hired a few new men. Cree imagined it was only a matter of time before he was taken into the woods and put down like a rabid dog. He welcomed the day. Until then, he got high and went over every second of the last year of his life and put a mental pin in all the places he had failed.

Cree knew where Nebraska was. He had followed Angel one day when he saw him loading groceries into his truck. Journey's old cabin was the perfect spot for him. He deserved the peace. Cree wouldn't darken his door. There was no forgiving his actions. Nebraska had loved him beautifully. Cree had taken a sledgehammer to all that flawlessness. He now lived the life he deserved.

"I'm not sure how freezing to death solves anything."

Cree's gaze moved King's way and then skirted away. They had nothing to say to each other. "Nothing to fix, is there?"

"Whatever. Fucking dumbass." King headed back inside, leaving Cree alone with his thoughts once more.

He fought a crazed smile. That was him. The fucking dumbass. His eyes closed. Cree's smile fell. His head spun from the smoke. Images of Nebraska filled his head. He no longer felt the cold. All he felt was done.

CHAPTER NINE

SPRING CAME, AND SO too did the restlessness. Each day, Nebraska would grab a throw blanket and walk the property. It was still chilly, but some flowers fought to bloom. Every day, he got a little farther away from the cabin. A few times, he made his way to the bench where he made his ill-fated plans with King. He would sit for hours and stare at nothing. Nebraska kept hoping his love for Cree would die. It didn't. He didn't feel as numb any longer. A few times, he had revisited that terrible final night in his mind. He saw some things a little more clearly now. They never talked. Not about Cree anyway. They talked about Nebraska's life all the time. Cree never broached the topic of his past. Hell, Nebraska hadn't known about his present either. His life had been closed to Nebraska. He realized, while he had told himself it was to keep him safe from Archer, that wasn't true. There was something broken inside Cree. Nebraska had never gotten a chance to help him. Now Nebraska was equally broken, and nothing mattered any longer.

Nebraska stared at the pond, mesmerized by the way the water rippled. He wondered how cold the water was and if he could walk into it and let the depths take him. Some people were born into this world to do nothing but hurt. Life kicked them and kicked them, stomping until there was nothing left. Nebraska was one of those people.

Something soft brushed his cheek. Nebraska's eyes fell closed. It felt like he walked into a dream. His eyes opened, and he wasn't hallucinating. A dandelion swept his cheek and appeared in front of his face. Nebraska's fingers automatically wrapped around the stem. Cree filled the spot beside him. He didn't look the same. His head was shaved, and he had lost a ton of weight. Cree's facial hair had gotten a bit wild. But Nebraska would know his scent anywhere, and everything he thought he would feel seeing Cree again didn't happen. He wasn't scared or angry. Nebraska just felt sad. He had thought they were so beautiful. What a starry-eyed child he had been.

With his elbows resting on his knees, Cree stared at the water. Nebraska stared at him. They didn't speak. Time passed. Neither of them moved. When his ass went numb, Nebraska stood. He headed toward the cabin without looking back.

"Will you meet me here again tomorrow?"

Nebraska didn't answer. He kept moving. Maybe he would come tomorrow. Probably not, though. That night, things were extra difficult. He felt the emptiness harder than usual. Several times, his eyes shot open, and his gaze darted to Cree's side of the bed. Then the pain would hit again when he remembered all he had lost.

The next morning, he paced for an hour before grabbing his throw blanket and heading for the door. When he opened it, he found a rose and a letter. Nebraska tucked both beneath the blanket against his chest. His feet carried him to the bench by the lake. It was empty. Nebraska wasn't surprised. A part of him had known Cree wouldn't show. For a few minutes, he stared at the water, working up the courage to open the letter. Finally, curiosity won.

Nebraska,

As much as I feel like this should be nothing but a huge, long apology, sometimes that's not enough. Words without change is gaslighting. I don't know if I can change.

Being with you, loving you, triggered something in me I didn't know how to control. You see, you're not the first time I've fallen in love.

For years, before Archer came along, I lived the worst sort of nightmare. I can't talk about that, but I can say that being saved by Archer changed me. He was everything I wasn't. He was charismatic and conniving enough to take over for my first boss, Wesley. Wesley was cold and cruel. Twisted. When Archer came to live with us, Wesley lost interest in me. I was too relieved to truly see why.

Like everyone else, I was completely enamored by Archer. I thought he loved me. Funnily enough, even while I knew he warmed Wesley's bed, I still couldn't stop wanting him. It tainted nothing for me. At least, that's what I thought at the time.

I thought, like me, Archer didn't have a choice. Wesley wanted him. He had to obey. Then Archer married Wesley and I learned I had just been... well, nothing, I suppose.

Still, I ignored the betrayal and my broken heart. He had still saved me from a terrible life, securing my loyalty forever. I honestly thought I didn't carry any scars from those days until I saw you with King. Everything felt the same. I couldn't do it again. I knew I didn't have the strength to watch you move from my heart to his when you've meant so much more to me than Archer ever did.

This excuses nothing. I never deserved you, but I still need you to know the whys. You deserve that. You're owed the peace of knowing it was never you. Not for a single second were you to blame. It's me.

I'm damaged. There isn't enough beauty in anyone or anything to fill my cracks. If anyone could fix me with love alone, it would be you. Some things are just too broken to be put back together. I'm one of those things. That doesn't mean I don't love you. It doesn't mean we weren't real. I'm just the devil to your angel. You're the light. I'm the dark, sucking life from everything I touch.

Maybe one day, you'll look back and not hate me. No matter what, you're the one for me. I'll love you until my dying breath. Please be at peace.

Cree

Nebraska went back to staring at the water. Cree was right. His explanation changed nothing. There was something completely different about the letter that was trying to squeeze the life from his chest. The note sounded like goodbye. There was only one way Archer would ever let him go, and it was the only outcome Nebraska couldn't endure.

It had taken every ounce of Cree's strength to stay away from the bench by the pond. Instead, he claimed his spot on their lounge and smoked. He stayed high more often than not. Cree couldn't decide if he chose to waste away until he didn't wake up any longer, or if he waited for some sign that it was time to eat that bullet. It didn't matter. The outcome was the same. He could no longer live with himself. Nebraska had once been all smiles and happy chatter. The life had left him too, and that was on Cree. Some mistakes were too big to take back.

When darkness fell and the sounds inside the house quieted, Cree headed inside. He swayed on his feet as he climbed the stairs. A chuckle nearly choked him. Maybe he would fall and break his neck. That was a third option he hadn't considered. As he reached his door, he couldn't grasp the doorknob. It kept running away and forcing him to catch it. Finally, it turned beneath his hand. He crossed the threshold and froze. Nebraska sat on his bed. He blinked, wondering if he hallucinated.

Nebraska held up a piece of paper. "Why does this sound like a suicide note?"

He sounded angry. Cree got a suspicion this wasn't a dream. He stepped inside the room and shut the door. His back fell against it as the floor rocked beneath him.

Nebraska sighed and climbed from the bed. "Come on. Let's get you to bed." He snagged Cree's hands and helped him cross the bucking floor to his bed. His ass hit the mattress so hard, he bounced. Nebraska went to work, undressing him. Something inside Cree that had been building for months broke. Tears filled his eyes.

"Just leave me. You deserve better than to be here right now. This is what I deserve."

Even through his tears, he saw Nebraska roll his eyes. "God. You sound just like my dad used to. If you want things to be different. If you want this to change, fucking work on it. Otherwise, this pity party doesn't mean shit. It just sounds like another addict who can't wait to abuse me again."

Cree cried harder. He hadn't shed a tear in his life he could remember. Now he couldn't stop. "You think I was abusive? Fuck. You really should just let me die. I can't live with that."

Nebraska peeled off Cree's shirt. While standing between Cree's knees, he gripped Cree's shoulders and held his stare. "No. If you really love me, then prove it. This isn't the man I fell in love with. You haven't been that guy for a while. But I know I didn't imagine him and I know you weren't pretending to be someone else. It was real. What we had was genuine and gorgeous. But no, I don't want the man you are right now, and I can't love the man you were at the end. Maybe I was wrong too. I don't know anymore. But you can't wipe the slate this way. You can only do more damage."

He pushed, tumbling Cree into bed. His eyelids were too heavy to stay up so he could focus on Nebraska. A blanket pulled across him. The bed dipped at his hip. Nebraska's fingers ran across his buzzed hair. "I still love you. Don't make me hate myself for that."

Oblivion carried Cree away, but he heard the words. He wouldn't let Nebraska hate himself. No matter what it took.

CHAPTER TEN

A WEEK AFTER TUCKING Cree into bed, Nebraska had given up on ever seeing him again. He wasn't at peace with that. His feelings didn't matter, though. They never had. Life would do what it wanted. Nebraska would survive or he wouldn't. He didn't think he had much of a say in the matter.

When the knock came, Nebraska expected it would be Archer or Angel. The last thing he saw coming was King on his doorstep. He, too, looked as if he had lost weight. There were dark circles under his eyes. A sad smile touched his lips as Nebraska opened the door. It fell every bit as quickly. "Hey."

"Hey." Nebraska didn't know how he felt, but he still stepped aside, silently inviting King inside. It wasn't his fault that things had gone to shit. Still, Nebraska didn't feel the same about anything any longer. He wasn't the same.

King shook his head. "I don't want to cause any more hurt. But I also couldn't leave without saying goodbye, and I'm sorry."

Nebraska's throat swelled. Tears burned at the back of his eyes. He realized he was wrong. Nebraska did feel the same. King was his best friend. Even knowing how it all ended, he wouldn't have changed the way he handled things. Nebraska would always protect his secret. He cleared his throat.

"Leave? Where are you going?"

King shifted from foot to foot. He looked like he no longer knew his place. So much hurt all around. The ugliness was cloying. "Archer is sending me away. I mean, it's another position that sounds necessary and honest on paper, but I know the deal. Cree's been with him longer. Things will never have any chance of going back to normal as long as I'm around."

Nebraska could see the hurt in his eyes. He was a guard dog dropped at the pound. Nowhere was home. Nebraska understood. "I need you." The words came out in a whisper, but Nebraska felt them in his soul. "You're my family. No matter what or where you go."

King looked away.

Nebraska saw the tears he fought not to shed. He cleared his throat but didn't look Nebraska's way again. "My number is the same. Use it if you need anything. No matter the time of day or what happens, I'll come."

It turned out being touch-starved was a state Nebraska couldn't adjust to. No matter how long he went without human contact, he still needed it. "Will you at least give me a hug before you go?"

Finally, King's gaze moved Nebraska's way again. They moved at the same time. For much longer than necessary, they held each other. King kissed his temple.

"You're my only family too. Please don't forget me or give up." Those words hurt more than Nebraska expected, because King was right. Nebraska did want to give up. It felt like time. He was too tired for his age. Nebraska felt like eighty instead of twenty. Maybe that was all he had in him. He supposed—soon enough—he would see.

For much longer than necessary, King sat in his car and stared at Nebraska's front door. He knew he needed to get going. Bryson waited for his arrival. All his things were packed. King couldn't force himself to put the car in gear. He felt the same way he had the day he had been sent to Archer. He felt like nothing. King was an asset. A piece of human property to be bartered and disposed.

He knew Archer's reasoning sounded plausible. Bryson worked with a senator they planted in New York on a land deal to build Archer's future warehouses. There were a ton of crazies out there when it came to politics. Death threats had been pouring in, bombarding Bryson. Archer needed to protect his plans. Bryson needed a guy under his roof. King was the logical choice. He knew better, though. King had disrupted Archer's peaceful household. He had to go. None of it really mattered, except Nebraska did.

Knowing Nebraska was a brisk walk away had kept King sane. In his heart, he had thought they could be friends again. Nebraska felt real—like his very first family member. He had nothing without that, and it had been stripped from him.

King's hand landed on the gearshift. He really had to go. The passenger side door opened, and Cree climbed inside. He didn't look King's way. His jaw was set in a hard line.

"I'm sorry."

King blinked. He hadn't expected that one. For a second, he had thought Cree intended to seize his last shot at killing King. He didn't know what to say, so he said nothing.

Cree's chest expanded on a deep breath. His shoulders relaxed a hair. "You were important to Nebraska. You *are* important to Nebraska. I shouldn't have ruined that. He deserves to have a friend and so do you." His intense gaze finally swung King's way and King realized he meant it. "Please don't disappear. I know I don't deserve anything, but I thought we were friends too before I destroyed everything. Plus, Nebraska needs you. It's not good for him to always be alone."

King drew a deep breath. He knew that took a lot for Cree to say. "Well, Bryson's place is only about forty-five minutes from here. I don't know what my time off will look like as his only employee. But I won't disappear. I promise."

Cree nodded. "If you want me to talk to Archer."

King shook his head. "It's done. I saw the contract. I've already changed hands. Bryson has already paid in full to buy me from Archer. A slave is a slave is a slave. You know how it is."

"I have some money saved. I could buy your freedom."

A sad smile pulled at King's lips. "Why? I'm nothing. You know that. I have no name or social security number. Not one that would hold up for long. What would I do? This is all I know."

Cree nodded and squeezed King's shoulder. "The offer stands if you ever change your mind. If nothing else, I can lean on Archer to bring you back. I'm kind of in the doghouse right now, but Archer would still listen."

"Don't worry about me. Go get your life back. Nothing will make me feel better than knowing Nebraska isn't alone. He's not as strong as he pretends, and he gave up everything just to be my friend. I can't live with that. No one else has ever cared about me like that."

Cree took another deep breath. "I don't think I'm what he needs, but I won't let him be alone either."

"That's all I can ask."

With a final nod, Cree climbed from the car. That was it. It was time for King to move on. Sometimes, there were no winners. Sometimes felt like always to him.

CHAPTER ELEVEN

EACH AND EVERY DAY, Cree longed for Nebraska. He had to wait until he was ready. There was no other way. He half expected the first time he turned up on Nebraska's doorstep, he would have already missed his chance. It wasn't like Nebraska couldn't have anyone he wanted. There were definitely better choices than Cree. Archer had been paying Nebraska for a while now. He could afford to leave them behind.

He swiped his sweaty palms on his jeans. His gaze stayed locked on the door. He didn't know if he could knock. Before he could decide, the door swung open. Nebraska looked put out.

"I got tired of waiting to see what you'd do."

Fuck. He was beautiful. "I still don't know."

A smile touched Nebraska's lips. "Would you like to come in?"

Would he? Damn, he was a mess. Finally, Nebraska's hand shot out. He snagged Cree's shirt and hauled him inside. Cree forced his gaze to focus on something other than Nebraska. He had rearranged the furniture.

"Things look different in here."

Nebraska shrugged. "I get bored a lot."

That was Cree's fault. "I want to say I'm sorry, since I know that's my fault, but my therapist says I need to work on that since it's a trauma response."

To his surprise, Nebraska became the one who looked uncomfortable. "I didn't have dinner planned or anything since I didn't know you were coming."

Cree nodded. "That's okay. I actually came by to ask if I could take you to dinner."

"I'd like that." Nebraska sounded genuine. That eased some tension in Cree's shoulders. Nebraska glanced around the room. "Um. Just let me grab my shoes."

"Do whatever you need." Cree shoved his hands in his pockets to hide the way they shook. He couldn't recall ever being this nervous. Everything rode on Nebraska giving him this chance. He didn't want to fail. Cree needed to be a better man for Nebraska. Their love meant everything to him, and he knew now that would never change for him. Months apart had dampened nothing. Cree's arms still ached to hold Nebraska. His chest felt empty without Nebraska's smiles. He couldn't live without his other half.

Cree watched as Nebraska put on his shoes and gathered his things. He finally headed back Cree's way. "Okay. I'm ready."

As much as Cree hated tearing his eyes away, he turned and opened the door. Nebraska followed him out, locking the door behind him. Cree headed for his

SUV and opened the passenger side door for Nebraska.

Nebraska flashed him a smile and climbed inside. He waited until Cree slid behind the wheel before saying anything. "You got a new SUV."

Cree focused on maneuvering his way down the long driveway before responding. He hated bringing up anything bad from the past almost immediately. "The other one had some triggering memories attached. I needed a change."

Nebraska didn't say anything.

Cree chanced a quick glance his way.

Nebraska looked thoughtful. Finally, he spoke. "It had some good memories too. You rescued me in that SUV."

"Not enough." Cree didn't know how to explain how some things felt very unsalvageable to him.

"I understand."

Cree imagined he did. He doubted—no matter what happened—that Nebraska would ever want to share their bedroom again. Cree had likely scarred Nebraska in a lot of ways he didn't deserve. His thoughts darkened. He knew he had to say something, because not talking had been their biggest downfall.

"I'm starting to feel like, if I was a better man, then I would leave you in peace."

Another round of silence met his confession. It was as if Nebraska picked through his words before finding the right ones. "Since I lost you, in the most horrific way, I don't have any peace to disturb."

That hurt Cree's chest. He genuinely wanted to fix them. Most of the time, that felt impossible. "I'm sorry."

A cute chuckle caressed his ears. "You're supposed to be working on not constant-ly apologizing."

"You're owed several."

"Hmm." Nebraska blew out a breath. "Maybe. Maybe not. Upon many months of reflection, I see all the ways I went wrong too. It was obvious you didn't feel confident in our relationship. Instead of doing whatever it took to reassure you, I decided I didn't want to be treated like an untrustworthy child, so I pushed back by doing what I wanted with no regard to the damage it did to us."

"You were right, though. You hadn't re-ally done anything to be treated like an untrustworthy child. King and you both deserved to have a friend."

From the corner of his eye, Cree saw Nebraska make a dismissive gesture. "It doesn't really matter now. We both made mistakes. Some were bigger than others. The damage is done. All we can do is move forward."

That was fair. Cree still wanted to grovel, though. But, at the end of the day, actions spoke louder than words. He needed to prove he could do better, or he didn't deserve Nebraska. "So, Mexican?"

"That sounds amazing." Cree heard the smile in Nebraska's voice. He hoped that meant they were headed in the right direction. Only time would tell. For now, he just wanted to be exactly where he was: with Nebraska.

Since Nebraska never went anywhere, he enjoyed looking at everything. There were sombreros on the wall mixed with an Aztec paint scheme. As curious as the restaurant made him, his gaze kept finding its way back to Cree. Cree stared at the menu on the table, as if scared to look anywhere else. Since Cree had gotten them takeout from here several times, Nebraska already knew what he wanted. He always got the same thing. They had already ordered drinks. Now all Nebraska had to focus on was them.

"What made you decide to shave your head?"

Cree's sexy blue gaze lifted and focused on Nebraska. "I don't know, really. Frustration combined with a driving need to change, I suppose."

Nebraska nodded. "It's nice."

"Your hair is getting thicker."

A chuckle escaped Nebraska. "It never gets longer. Only thicker and curlier." He shrugged. "I can't drive. Not that I have a car anyhow, and I don't have people around anymore who cut hair." While living with Cree, there had never been a need for him to go anywhere. Professionals were in and out of the house all day, providing services so they didn't have to risk their safety by going anywhere. Living alone meant giving up housekeepers and cooks. It meant no haircuts and a dozen other things. Nebraska depended on Nebraska now. In some ways, it was preferable. In other ways, it was isolating.

"If you want, after we eat, I can take you to get it cut. I'm sorry I've been too self-involved to realize how much you're missing because of me."

A smile exploded across Nebraska's face. "You're apologizing again."

Cree stayed serious. "I'm sorry. I love you more than anything in this world, and every day I have to wake up knowing I hurt you and failed you. Apologizing for that isn't a habit I think I can break."

Nebraska took a breath. He didn't know how to respond. As much as he wanted to say he loved Cree too, he couldn't risk Cree using that love against him again. He wasn't ready. Thankfully, their server appeared, saving him.

"Are you ready to order?"

Nebraska looked Cree's way.

Cree shrugged. "I'm ready if you are."

With a nod, Nebraska ordered, and then listened while Cree did. When they were alone again, they fell into a companionable silence. After a few minutes of sipping their drinks and avoiding each other's stare, something odd happened. They both reached across the table at the same time and joined hands. A shaky breath escaped Nebraska. He missed being touched. Their meal came, and they ate without talking about anything heavy. The food disappeared. Way too soon for Nebraska's heart, they were headed back to the SUV. He let Cree take him for a haircut just so he could have more time.

By the time Cree walked him to his door, a sadness settled into Nebraska's soul. He knew their time had ended. Cree wouldn't try to stay, and Nebraska wasn't ready to make the offer. Everything felt tenuous, as if it hung by a string.

They stopped at the door. Cree shoved his hands in his pockets. "Home safe and sound. Thank you for going with me."

"Thank you for the invitation."

Neither of them moved.

Cree broke first. "Well, I guess I should let you get back to it."

Nebraska had no idea what that meant, but he understood they were equally unsure. "Okay. Thanks again for everything."

Cree nodded.

Nebraska stuck his key in the door.

"So, I was thinking."

"Yes?" Nebraska turned back Cree's way with more than a little hope in his heart.

Cree still looked uncomfortable. "Maybe I can come by tomorrow and start teaching you how to drive."

A smile exploded through Nebraska. "That would be amazing."

Cree nodded again. "Okay. Sounds good. Maybe around one. Does that sound good?"

Nebraska nodded. "I'll be ready."

Cree took a step back. "Okay. I guess I'll see you then."

"See you then." Nebraska forced himself to go inside and shut the door. He lost the battle against looking out the window. Nebraska watched Cree head back to his SUV. Cree sat in the driveway longer than necessary. Nebraska couldn't decide if he wanted Cree to jump out and come back. Finally, the SUV moved. Nebraska took a step back.

He eyed the cabin that was devoid of life. The loose hairs on his skin got him moving. He needed a shower to wash away the itchiness.

Nebraska headed for the bathroom. He fired the shower to life and undressed while the water heated. Steam filled the air, making Nebraska realize he had gotten lost in his head for a minute. His gaze accidentally collided with the mirror. He didn't look at himself often. Nebraska supposed his hair looked better now. It wasn't as fluffy and wild. He had never liked what he saw when he looked at himself. Nebraska was too skinny. He didn't like his nose. His dad had broken it too many times. There was a scar through his left eyebrow. Hair wouldn't grow there. He had an ugly, jagged scar on his chest where his dad had tried cutting his heart out with a broken beer bottle one night. He was a roadmap of unfortunate memories. Too many times, he had wondered what Cree saw in him. Nebraska's chest expanded on a deep breath. Listening to Cree's apologies had been hard, because Nebraska knew the truth. He was every bit as broken.

Nebraska headed inside the shower, determined to wash away the ugly thoughts. He closed his eyes and dipped his head beneath the water. Hot streams rolled down his skin. Cree's face filled his mind. A sudden memory hit. Hot water and soap had streamed between their bodies. Cree had held Nebraska's stare as he washed every inch of Nebraska's skin. His chest filled with something he couldn't name. The way Cree had watched him still heated his skin. His cock stirred. He had never felt sexier or more powerful than when Cree looked at him. There was always so much heat. So much passion. He could feel Cree's desire. It was empowering in a way Nebraska hadn't experienced before him.

Nebraska's hand slid down his body. He kept his eyes closed as he palmed his erection. Damn. He missed Cree's hands. Nebraska craved Cree's mouth. Cree did things with that perfect mouth that Nebraska hadn't known was possible before him. Nebraska stroked, wishing it was

Cree touching him. He had gone months without touching himself. Nebraska had been too raw. Any time his body stirred, the shame hit. Not this time. This time, he saw Cree's face in his head and longed for Cree's huge, hard body. When they had been together, he had spent a ridiculous amount of time picturing himself riding that cock. He hadn't appreciated how perfect it had been fucking those abs instead. Nebraska missed the times he had ridden Cree's thigh while Cree held his stare and praised him. He stroked himself as he remembered the heated kisses. The sweat. The love. Nebraska pressed his forehead against the shower wall. His eyes burned even as his body begged for release. Pressure climbed his shaft while loss filled his soul. Tears fell as Nebraska came. He pumped out every drop while he silently pleaded for the pain to end. Nebraska wanted the old Cree back. He wanted to be healed.

CHAPTER TWELVE

CREE PRESENTED HIMSELF AT exactly one o'clock. He had barely slept from over-thinking and the excitement. Plus, he had never gotten used to his empty bed. Cree didn't get the chance to knock. He was halfway to the door when it opened, and Nebraska stepped outside. Cree immediately knew something had shifted be-tween them. Nebraska was all genuine smiles. He looked happy to see Cree. The air felt lighter as Nebraska skipped his way.

"I'm going to drive."

Cree laughed at Nebraska's excitement. "You know, most people are nervous about getting on the road for the first time."

Nebraska shrugged. "Technically, it's not my very first time. I took driver's ed in school. So I've driven like four times for maybe ten minutes each."

"That's good. Then you know how to get started." He passed his keys Nebraska's way.

With a squeal, Nebraska raced to the driver's side. Cree shook his head and followed at a slower pace. He liked watching Nebraska. When they were piled into the

SUV, Nebraska turned serious. He made a show of adjusting the mirrors and seat. Cree sighed. It would take him forever to get everything right again. It was worth it to see Nebraska happy.

Nebraska turned bright eyes his way, looking excited. "Are you ready? Buckle your seatbelt."

Cree pulled his seatbelt over his shoulder. He didn't usually wear one in case he had to bail out and kick ass. Cree wanted Nebraska to feel in control, so he did what he asked.

Finally, Nebraska put the SUV in gear. With his tongue between his teeth, Nebraska slowly turned the SUV around in the driveway and headed for the road. He moved extra slowly and sat too close to the wheel. Cree said nothing. It was important Nebraska felt comfortable. Nebraska sat at the mouth of the driveway and watched for cars. They didn't get much traffic on this road, since it was mostly Archer's property, but they got deliveries and such.

"Good job not taking it for granted that no one was coming." Cree tried being encouraging.

Nebraska smiled as he eased out onto the road. Cree's gaze never wavered from him. If he made Nebraska uncomfortable, he didn't say anything. Cree imagined he was too hyperfocused on the road to notice. Nebraska creeped his way to Archer's place. He pulled into the driveway only long enough to turn around and head back again.

"You're doing great."

Nebraska never stopped smiling. He pulled back into his driveway and headed for the house. Panic hit Cree from nowhere. "Are you done already? We can stay out as long as you'd like."

"I think that's good for today. It's already almost one thirty and I haven't had lunch. I didn't want to eat without you, and I know you. You haven't eaten since last night."

Cree's shoulders relaxed. "Oh. Okay. What did you have in mind?"

Nebraska flashed him a smile as he put the SUV in park. "I'm making us lunch."

"All right." Cree didn't know Nebraska knew how to cook, but he was game. As long as he got to stay in Nebraska's company, he would do anything.

Together, they headed inside. Side by side, they took off their shoes. Nebraska set Cree's keys on the table and headed for the kitchen. Cree followed.

"What's on the menu and can I help?"

Nebraska motioned toward a stool at the island in the center of the kitchen. "Just sit. I'm trying something new."

Cree did as instructed.

Nebraska moved to the refrigerator and grabbed two grape sodas. He sat one in front of Cree. Cree popped the tab, but his gaze never left Nebraska. "So you haven't had any trouble getting what you need, right? I can go to the store for you anytime you want. Just send me a list."

"It's been fine." Nebraska opened the door, showing a full pantry. He grabbed a few things and shut the door. "I've been doing jobs for Archer and he's ridiculously generous. I've also mastered the skill of getting things delivered."

"Archer isn't being generous. Whatever you do for him makes him a million times more money than he gives you. He's buying your silence."

Nebraska shrugged. "It's not like I'm going anywhere or have anything else to offer. Working ten minutes here and there for gangster bucks is way better than any prospects I had for my future."

"I just don't want you to have any illusions. There's a reason this cabin is empty."

Nebraska pulled a rotisserie chicken from the fridge and started shredding it. "Since you brought it up, tell me about it.

I'm super fascinated. It's been fun digging through his things. There're some crazy interesting things here, but his clothes are still in the closet and dresser. His toothbrush is still in the bathroom. It was like a time capsule when I walked in here."

"This place belonged to Journey. He was Archer's last tech guy."

Nebraska nodded while keeping his gaze locked on his task. "I'm not surprised. There're some impressive computer components here. I could hack the pentagon with the system he left behind. Is he dead?"

Nebraska didn't sound scared. Of course, people like them didn't expect to live long or die well. "No. Archer is not the only powerful man out there. In fact, he's a small fish compared to some of the other players in the US. It seems Journey's husband is friends with one of the biggest. Archer was warned to let Journey go so he could be with his husband free and clear. He did, but Journey had to leave with only the clothes on his back."

"What's his husband like? Is he involved in dirty money too?"

A bark of laughter burst from Cree. "That depends on what you consider dirty. He owns the biggest porn production company in the US."

That got Nebraska's attention. He looked Cree's way. "Lucky guy."

Cree snorted. "Which one? Journey or Chad?"

Nebraska's eyebrows rose. "Chad? That's unfortunate in this day and age. I meant Journey. He got to marry the man he loves. That makes this time capsule twice as special. It's his sacrifice."

That wasn't what Cree expected. He should have, though. Nebraska was a romantic. It hit Cree. That was what he should have tried harder to be. He should have had candlelight dinners and spread rose petals on the bed. Cree should have drawn bubble baths and bought jewelry. He should have gotten down on one knee and begged for forever.

A plate appeared in front of Cree. He blinked. Cree had spaced out, lost in his thoughts, and missed the prep work. It was chicken salad. He could see walnuts and grapes. "This looks delicious."

Nebraska smiled like it was the highest of compliments. "I enjoy making stuff. Since I've been ordering whatever I want, I've gotten to experiment and have fun with it. I'm surprisingly good at it, I think."

Cree took a bite and savored the deliciousness before he responded. "This is amazing. Why did you sound surprised at your talent? I think you're amazing at everything you touch."

Nebraska took a bite. He didn't respond, but his blush told Cree he was happy. Cree wanted to be the person who built Nebraska up instead of tearing him down. This was important to him. He had to put in the work.

"I'm glad you're happy here. That's all I've ever wanted for you."

"It's quiet." He looked around, as if uncomfortable again. Finally, he met Cree's stare. "All I ever wanted was to be your soft space. Making you happy was the best part of me. It was the first time I felt like I mattered at all. So, yeah. I guess all I ever wanted was for you to be happy too."

"Go to therapy with me." The words were out before he could stop. Since it was too late, he continued. "I do online sessions and I had one last night. We were going over my day, and my therapist said we should think about doing some sessions together and apart." Cree shrugged. "I don't know. It seems to help. I want us to be better."

Nebraska nodded. "Okay."

"Okay," Cree repeated. He went back to eating. Again, it was a step in the right direction. He would take it.

After lunch, they went for a walk. Cree didn't rush away, thankfully. He stayed after their walk and they talked about nothing, but it felt like everything. When dinner rolled around, Cree helped him cook. They ate at the island again. This time, the tension was higher. Their gazes kept meeting and then sliding away. Nebraska recognized the heat that boiled between them.

After they ate, Cree washed the dishes. Nebraska had tried to convince him just to put them in the dishwasher. Since Cree was adamant, Nebraska let him have his way. As he watched, he was glad he hadn't put up a fight. It was a sexy sight, watching him dry dishes and put them away. Before Nebraska realized what he would do, his body molded against Cree's back. He kissed him between the shoulder blades and held tight. Cree stood completely still, as if he feared breaking the spell. Nebraska couldn't move away. Cree's warmth felt too real. He didn't want to rush. Nebraska was fucking terrified. But he also loved Cree and he couldn't control that.

"I want to turn around and hold you, but I don't want to scare you."

Nebraska hid a smile against Cree's back. "I'm not afraid."

Cree turned. His arms encircled Nebraska. Nebraska inhaled, savoring the scent of Cree's cologne. Cree kissed the top of Nebraska's head. Nebraska turned his face up without a single care. It was second nature to seek Cree's kisses. Their lips met. For a moment, they simply clung while Nebraska's heart tried doing cartwheels. Then his lips parted as Cree's tongue slid across his bottom lip. Still, their kiss stayed soft, seeking. His feet left the floor as Cree lifted him higher. Nebraska wrapped his legs around Cree's waist. Cree carried him to the island and set him on top. Nebraska imagined it didn't hurt his back as much. He was ridiculously smaller than Cree.

Cree pulled away enough to press his forehead against Nebraska's. They stayed like that. Cree kept his eyes closed while Nebraska couldn't get enough of staring.

"I'm so in love with you. No matter what. That won't change."

Nebraska drew an unsteady breath at Cree's confession. He felt the same. This wouldn't die. Even if he never saw Cree again, their love would still be the first thing he thought about when he woke up in the morning and his last thought before he fell asleep. "I don't know exactly how to fix us. But I know I love you and I have to try."

Cree's lips found his mouth again.

Nebraska understood their confessions had changed something between them, but he wasn't sure what yet. All he knew was he couldn't let this end. "Stay with me tonight."

CHARITY PARKERSON

"I don't want to ruin things."

"Then don't say no."

Cree's hands moved to Nebraska's waist. His lips skimmed Nebraska's as he drew Nebraska's shirt up his body. He pulled away and Nebraska lifted his arms so Cree could steal his shirt. Nebraska stole his chance to divest Cree of his shirt too. Things moved slow. They went back to kissing while Cree stroked Nebraska's back and sides, as if he couldn't get enough. Nebraska's hands went to Cree's belt.

Cree backed away. "I need you to be sure."

Nebraska held his stare. "I'm sure."

With a nod, Cree lifted Nebraska from the counter. They stripped each other in the kitchen before Cree carried him to the couch. He sat with Nebraska straddling his lap. With their erections between them, they kissed and touched. Time passed with no meaning. Every time Nebraska got carried away, moving against Cree, Cree slowed things down, drawing things out.

By the time Nebraska was ready to scream, sweat coated their skin. Cree stroked their cocks while Nebraska moved against him. He gasped for air, reaching for release. Cree kissed his throat while Nebraska begged.

"Please. I want to come all over you. I need it."

Cree pumped faster.

Nebraska turned wild. He was half insane with desire. When he finally blew, a cry tore from him. Cree moaned against his throat.

"Fuck. I love you. I can't do life without you. Please love me back."

Nebraska forced Cree to meet his stare. His expression nearly made Nebraska come again. He looked aroused and completely enamored. "I love you. You don't have to be afraid. I won't let you be alone." Nebraska didn't know what he promised exactly, but they weren't done. They would never be done.

Darkness enveloped them. Under the covers, in Nebraska's bed, they held on for dear life. Cree could practically feel the way they fought for each other—like it was a tangible thing. He had expected it to take months to get this far. Cree had been prepared to wait. He would never give up. Yet here they were, and Cree couldn't let go. He understood how fucking lucky he was that Nebraska let him touch him again.

"Can I ask you something?"

Cree kissed Nebraska's temple. He answered between kisses. "Of course."

Nebraska hesitated, as if he didn't know where to start or he was uncomfortable. Cree waited. He knew Nebraska was too brave to hold back. Finally, he blew out a breath as if finding his courage. "Is there a reason you... ugh." He tried again. "Why did you only touch me that one time like you did that last night?"

Fuck. He didn't want to answer, but he did. "I never wanted making love to you to hurt. No matter how much prep you put in, there's always some pain involved. I just wanted things to stay beautiful. As long as I make you fly, I'd rather not do that."

Nebraska was quiet longer than Cree wanted. He wished he'd stayed that way when he spoke. "So, it was only meant to punish me."

It wasn't a question. Nebraska had obviously settled a debate in his mind. "No." The denial immediately felt wrong. "Maybe. I don't know. When I saw you were at a hotel and I thought you were with King, it just broke me. I don't think

I've ever hurt that much, and I didn't know where to go with it. God, I just... yeah. I guess I wanted to make you hurt the way I did. But then I woke up, and you were gone. King and I almost tore each other apart. I put a gun to Archer's head. It wasn't until I was alone, and I put that same barrel to my head, that it really hit me how far I had gone off the ledge. I don't know if you really understand how you're all I have. No one prepared me for how to lose you."

Nebraska rolled. He kept coming until he straddled Cree's body and draped him like a blanket. Nebraska settled in—like he intended to stay there all night. He pressed his ear to Cree's chest. "I don't think you understand. I would rather rip out my heart than hurt you." He sniffed. A tear hit Cree's chest. "And I'd rather die than have anyone else touch me."

Cree ached all the way to his soul. He didn't want Nebraska to cry. Cree wanted to always be Nebraska's happiness. One way or another, it would happen. Cree would devote his entire life to spoiling Nebraska. Never again would he shed a tear as long as Cree walked this earth. That was a vow. Nebraska would see.

CHAPTER THIRTEEN

ONE DAY, CREE CAME for dinner and didn't leave. Nebraska had no complaints. They continued working on his driving until Archer presented him with a license. Really, it was the best Nebraska could hope for, since he had no access to his important documents. All of that had been left behind.

Two months after Cree moved in, he showed up with a huge box, looking insecure. Nebraska stopped in the middle of making a cake to investigate. "Why do you look like that? That's not an empty box to leave me with, is it?" Nebraska didn't really believe that. He just wanted to snap Cree out of his weirdness.

Cree shifted from foot to foot. "No. I would never do that. But I am worried you might ask me to leave once you see what's in this box."

Nebraska's curiosity doubled. "What did you do?"

Cree set the box on the island. "Well, I kind of ruined your birthday and you never got the gifts I bought you. Plus, we missed Christmas together too, and I bought you gifts then as well. I've kept them this whole time, but I'm worried you won't accept them. The last thing

I want is to hurt you by triggering bad memories."

He always tried so hard. Nebraska couldn't possibly do anything but adore him. He smiled brighter than he actually felt. Truthfully, Nebraska feared he very well might fall apart at the sight of those packages. "Let's see them."

Cree still looked unsure, but he reached inside the box. "I unwrapped everything, hoping that eased your anxiety." Nebraska appreciated that. Cree pulled out a stuffed white dog with a leash in its mouth. "First, I got you the electronic dog you said you begged Santa for and didn't get."

"Oh my God." Nebraska took the dog from Cree. It was exactly the one he had wanted at seven. There was a comb and a pink collar. It was still in the box even though they didn't make them anymore. He didn't know where Cree found the puppy, but he loved it. Nebraska hugged the box to his chest. "Thank you. It's perfect."

Obviously bolstered by Nebraska's reaction, he pulled out the next gift. "This is because I need to see you in it." Cree passed him a velvet box.

Nebraska set the dog aside and opened the box. He gasped. The reaction was completely beyond his control. A platinum and diamond necklace stared up at him. It was bolo style, with one side being a strand of diamonds. "This is... I'm beyond words. I love it."

Cree helped him put it on before moving on to the next gift. Nebraska stared at his chest, admiring the necklace until Cree shook something at him. He looked up. It was a key fob. "This was your Christmas gift."

Nebraska's brow furrowed. "What's that?"

Cree smiled. "It's for your car. It's in the driveway."

Nebraska moved to the front door on autopilot. He opened it to find a red Toyota Highlander. Nebraska's jaw dropped. "Are you kidding me?"

Strong arms engulfed him. Cree spoke against his ear. "It's a good car. It should last you a long time."

"Holy shit." Nebraska didn't know what else to say. Part of him wanted to rush outside and inspect every detail, but nothing felt real.

"Shut the door. There's more."

Nebraska turned. "More? What else could there be?"

Cree smiled. "I missed Valentine's Day too."

Shock rendered Nebraska mute. He followed Cree back to the kitchen on wooden legs. "There are a few birthday gifts in here I missed too. A couple of gift cards to places you like to get food delivered. I had gotten you several candies, but I had to throw those out. They went out of date."

All Nebraska could do was stand there and blink. Then Cree turned. He held an open velvet box with a diamond ring inside. "Then there's this." He moved as if to go down on one knee. "All I could think about when we were apart was how I should've—"

"Yes," Nebraska said before Cree made it to the floor.

Cree froze. It was obvious he didn't know how to react. "Don't you want me to—"

"No. The answer is yes."

A smile exploded across Cree's face. The distance between them disappeared. Nebraska clutched Cree's shirt with one hand, hanging on for dear life, while Cree slipped the ring on his left hand. For a moment, Nebraska could only stare at the ring of diamonds on his finger. Then Cree touched his chin. Nebraska lifted his gaze. Cree's mouth touched his.

"I love you," Nebraska whispered against his lips. All the bad disappeared. It was like the promise of an amazing future gave him the fresh start he needed. All Nebraska felt was happiness and love. He wouldn't let it end.

The pure joy and shock each gift had brought Nebraska was everything Cree wanted in life. All the gifts had just been things, but they were from Cree's heart. He wanted to give Nebraska the world. Their kiss turned heated faster than expected. He hadn't meant to go there. His body didn't care. They had always been explosive together.

Someone knocked on the front door. Cree groaned. He didn't want to stop.

Nebraska pulled away and held up one finger. "I'll be right back. Whoever it is, I'll get rid of them."

Cree followed him to the door. He couldn't help it. His body gravitated toward his other half.

Nebraska opened the door. "Oh. Hey."

He heard Archer's voice. "Please ask Cree to step outside."

Something dark raised its head inside of Cree. He had been doing really well, but something about Archer's words made him feel like it was all about to be ripped away. He headed for the door. Since he had moved Nebraska's car today, he knew Archer had to know now for certain that Cree had moved in with Nebraska permanently. Archer could shut them down with one order. Cree wouldn't comply and he'd die. Either way, things might have come to an end just as they were beginning.

Cree stepped outside and pulled the door closed behind him without ever meeting Nebraska's gaze. He couldn't let his baby know anything was wrong. Cree tried to play it cool. "Hey, what's up?"

Archer's chest expanded on a deep breath. Cree braced for the worst. Archer motioned toward the new SUV in the driveway. "I see you finally gave Nebraska his gift."

Cree nodded. "It was time. I mean, it was a risk, but still, it was time."

For a moment, Archer stared at some point over Cree's shoulder. Finally, his gaze slid Cree's way. Cree's shoulders relaxed. He knew this side of Archer. It was the side only he—and he imagined Angel—got to see. "I have a few things to get off my chest."

"Okay." They were always straight with each other, even when it was ugly.

"I like Nebraska. I think he actually has what it takes to keep you in line. Let me just say that right off the bat."

"But?"

Archer shook his head. "There's no but. I've just been thinking about some things since Nebraska left. It's eating at me. You've been my... I don't know. Best friend, I guess. For a long time. I know I played a huge role in fucking you up. You still didn't hesitate to help me win Angel back. Yet I still never said, I'm sorry."

"I'm not." Even Cree was surprised as the confession fell from his lips. He smiled as he realized how true the words were. "Without you, who knows where I would've ended up? I've told you dozens of times, but you saved me from a horrible life. Not only will I never forget that, but I'll also always love you. You *are* my best friend. I'm sorry I haven't been much of one lately. I guess I just learned my breaking point."

Archer nodded. "I get it. That's why I've left you alone to figure things out. Without Nebraska, there's no beauty in your world. It's the same for me with Angel. Unfortunately, it seems people like us have to lose the people we care about the most to learn how to care properly. But

I love you too. You're closer to me than blood. With that said, if I find out you're fucking up again, I'll drag your ass out of here. We gave Nebraska this place as a haven. Make it a good home."

Cree felt too much. It was like once he let his walls down for Nebraska, everyone crawled in. Before he could stop himself, he hugged Archer. To his surprise, Archer hugged him back.

"You better marry that boy. He's earned it."

Cree laughed. "He's already said yes."

Archer laughed. "Good. That's good. I'll let you get back to him. Just let us know when we can witness this wedding."

"I will." Cree watched Archer head to his truck. He waited until Archer climbed behind the wheel before he went back inside.

Nebraska stood in the middle of the living room, rubbing his arm and looking nervous. "Is everything okay?"

Cree nodded. "Damn right it is. I have you."

As far as Cree was concerned, that was all that needed to be said. He snatched Nebraska off his feet and tossed him over his shoulder. Cree headed for their bedroom, wearing a huge grin. For once, he was the winner. This one time, he hadn't failed. Cree planned to keep Nebraska in bed for the rest of the day and night. They had an engagement to celebrate.

CHAPTER FOURTEEN

ON NEBRASKA'S TWENTY-FIRST BIRTHDAY, and in front of everyone they loved, Nebraska listened to Cree repeat his wedding vows strong and clear. It was the best way imaginable to break his birthday curse. He smiled so much, his face hurt. Nebraska declined all the champagne offered to him. He would never be his dad. That was his vow.

They had married in Archer's huge living room. Angel and King had done the decorations. The day felt so surreal. His head spun by the time they made it to their hotel room for the night. They would leave tomorrow for a month-long European vacation. Nebraska was so excited, he could barely contain it. He was one hundred percent certain he wouldn't sleep.

Cree kissed his neck as he peeled away the layers of Nebraska's white tuxedo. He had almost decided against the color since his blond hair usually left him washed out when he wore white. King had added just enough black embellishments on the outfit to balance things. Since Nebraska trusted King on all things fashion-related, he hadn't fought against the design. The way Cree couldn't seem to get him out of it quickly enough, Nebraska assumed it had the desired effect.

Nebraska couldn't stop touching Cree. He never got enough of the beautiful body hidden beneath Cree's black tux.

"Goddamn. I love you, Mr. Erebus."

Nebraska's eyes fell closed. No one would ever know how glad he was to be rid of his father's last name. "I love you too. Say my name again."

Cree smiled against his skin. Nebraska felt his happiness. "Mr. Nebraska Erebus."

"Mmm. So sexy."

"Damn right you are."

Nebraska had to have him. The feeling never lessened. From the first night they shared a bed and didn't touch, this craving had become a full-blown addiction.

Nebraska dropped to his knees. Zero shame.

Cree lifted him from the floor. "No. You're not bruising your knees tonight. You'll blow me in bed like a good boy. Oh, and I also plan to be sucking your dick while you suck mine."

Yes. Nebraska wanted that. He tore at Cree's clothes. In no time, he was fucking Cree's face while choking on Cree's cock. He already knew this was only the first of many orgasms Cree would give him tonight. The hot suction of his mouth had Nebraska already ready for more. He wanted to spit cum all over Cree's body.

At the oddest moment, and like a truck, reality hit Nebraska. This was his family now. It was good and strong and kind.

Loving. It was so fucking loving—like nothing he had ever known. He slowed down and treasured his gift. They had the rest of their lives. For once, Nebraska didn't need to fight so desperately to horde every happy memory. He knew there would be more. Cree would never fail him.

Keep an eye out for the next Damaged Devils, *Devoted Sinner*.

Please consider leaving a review at the retailer where you purchased this book. Reviews really help with a book's visibility, which allows me to continue writing more stories. Thank you, Charity.

About the Author

CHARITY PARKERSON IS AN award-winning and multi-published author with several companies. Born with no filter from her brain to her mouth, she decided to take this odd quirk and insert it in her characters. One of her greatest loves is writing morally gray characters. You'll find them scattered throughout her hundreds of titles.

*Eight-time Readers' Favorite Award Winner

*2015 Passionate Plume Award Finalist

*2013 Reviewers' Choice Award Winner

*2012 ARRA Finalist for Favorite Paranormal Romance

*Five-time winner of The Mistress of the Darkpath

Connect with her online:

*Sign up for her newsletter: https://sendfox.com/charityparkerson

*Join her readers' group on Facebook: http://bit.ly/CharitysTribe

*Website: https://www.charityparkerson.com

*A list of her social media accounts and giveaways all in one place: http://hy.page/charityparkerson

CONTENT

CONTENT WARNING: DAMAGED DEVILS is a dark romance series that deals with dark subjects. There is murder, sexual assault, abuse, kidnapping, some dubcon, and power dynamic relationships. These are anti-hero books. They won't be for everyone.